Also By Nanette L. Avery
Out of the Rabbit Hutch
Orphan in America
A Curious Host
Sixty Jars in A Pioneer Town
The Fortune Teller and Other Short Works
Once Upon A Time Words
My Mother's Tattoo and Other Stories for Kids
First Aid for Readers

THE COLONY

THE
COLONY

Nanette L. Avery

The Colony

Printed in the United States of America

Print ISBN: 978-1-54399-191-8

eBook ISBN: 978-1-54399-192-5

For

Don Carrot, Bicky, and all the others
Thanks for the memories

PREFACE

THEY WEREN'T ALWAYS friends, not until they found out they had something in common. And then they started to wonder; how many others were like them; others with the same secret. That's how it started, with a secret, and then it grew into The Colony.

CHAPTER 1

*I*F YOU ARE *reading this, then you know I didn't make anything up. I can wait for you, but not too long, and then you won't find me. You don't have to prepare anything or prove anything to me. Just bring yourself, I'll know if you are telling the truth. How do you know I'm not lying ... you don't; but then you're an expert on liars; we both are. Flush this down the toilet when you finish reading it. 5:00 p.m. at The Bell Jar.*

There was a crumpling of paper right before the toilet flushed. He watched the water swirl around the bowl as it was getting sucked down the drain. "Coward," he said right before the words bell jar were being tossed around his head. He unraveled the paper and read it again. *"I'll know you are telling the truth..."* He rolled the note into a ball, and this time, tossed it into the toilet. The ink immediately started to bleed, and a faint trail of blue began making a squiggly pattern. He bent over and with his finger, moved the paper. The trail followed.

"What's taking you so long! There's other people in this house you know who need to take a shit!"

The toilet flushed. "Be right out, just washing my hands." *I can wait for you but not too long...*

* * *

THEY USED TO visit the fishing port where his mother grew up. The boardwalk was long and wooden, and underneath were mounds of dried seaweed, finely crushed pieces of shells, and sand. The tide rolled in twice a day, bringing with it the smell of diesel and bait. After work, his father often went to the dogfights, which nobody liked to talk about except when he came home with presents and beer. *5:00 pm tomorrow at The Bell Jar. It did say tomorrow?*

"What's a bell jar?"

"Don't talk with yer mouth full."

"A bell jar?"

He kicked his sister's chair. "I'm not talkin to you."

"What did ya kick my chair for?"

"I didn't kick your chair; I was asking Mom a question."

"Both of you stop fighting!"

"I just wanted to know what a bell jar was."

"Stupid, don't you know what it is?"

"If I knew I wouldn't be asking Mom."

"Ask me what?"

"What's a bell jar?"

"Still think it's a stupid question, what do you want to know for?"

"Stop your bickering. And use a napkin, why do you think we buy them!"

He wiped his mouth and swallowed. The sister stuck her tongue out at him. "He's askin you what's a bell jar." She patted her mouth with the napkin and grinned like a cat.

"A book."

"A book? He wanted to know what a bell jar is."

"For Christ's sake, I heard him. It's a book. The name of a book, *The Bell Jar*. Now, eat your damn supper and let me have some peace."

"Can we have some dessert?"

"Yes, but not too much. I'm going out."

"Out?"

"Yes, to get a bell jar."

They all laughed.

She had lost weight, and her dress hung on her like a curtain on a rod. She wadded up some tissues and stuffed her bra. The cigarette rested between her fingers, but before she took a drag, she leaned into the mirror and slid the mascara wand over her lashes. Her eyes met the boy's. "If anyone comes to the door, don't open it." She sucked on the cigarette and then, with a long generous exhale, let it out through her nostrils. She saw his reflection nod. "Just tell them to come back tomorrow, after 10. No," she amended, "after 11. Got that?" She twirled around on the stool and leaning over, dropped the lit cigarette into the soda can. "Now give mummy a kiss, and don't fight with your sister."

He thought suddenly of his neighbor and hoped the man wouldn't come by. "What if the dragon guy comes by."

"Which dragon guy?"

"You know, from next door?"

"What did I tell you to do?" She turned back to the mirror, and before putting on her lipstick, she licked her lips.

"Don't let him in."

"That's right. I said, 'don't let anyone in, no one.' That means no one. I don't care who they are or what they're sellin' or buyin.'" She smiled at the boy and rotated the lipstick tube. "I feel like wearing 'red-hot momma.'" But she screwed up her nose and slid 'pink paradise' over her lips several times, so it blended into the peanut shell wrinkles. She had tied her hair back with a barrette, and it lay across her shoulder like a squirrel tail. The boy stood and watched, but his mind was not on her shit. *Meet me at The Bell Jar.*

"I'll be late. Lock the door behind me and tell your sister what I said. If she gives you any crap," the mother thought for a moment and grinned, "she's a good girl. Let her watch T.V. after ice cream." He nodded. The idea of being in charge let him no longer feel like a small shrimp of a kid. He sauntered over to the bed and sat down.

"What the hell do you think you're doing?" She had broken the moment with just the whip of her tongue.

"Nothin', just thought I'd wait for you." He noticed a change in her expression as her eyebrows pinched together.

"Well, get your little butt up and wait outside!" She took a long hard look at the boy and picked up the wine glass teetering on a stack of magazines. The woman smelled strongly of cologne and mint mouthwash. He blinked, but she was still there.

"Well?" she said.

He raised himself and moseyed out but not before noticing the paper bag. There was no point in pretending. She was a bitch.

It was a medium-size house, three bedrooms, a kitchen, living room, small dining area, and a garden. The only set of stairs led to the basement where the furnace and washing machine lived. In the summer, the fenced yard grew crabgrass and dandelions, and in the autumn the oak tree let its leaves fall. The front porch was a good place to watch the neighbors or let the neighbors see you. It was the only house the boy and the girl ever lived in. There was no mortgage or overdue taxes, only the water bill and electric came every month on the first. When it rained the porch leaked, but other than that it was a sturdy place to live. There was a sheltered garden with plants growing in a long room at the end of the hallway with a padlocked door. Aluminum light fixtures hung from chains like an auto parts store, functional and unaesthetically pleasing. There was no night or day, just on and off from these fluorescent stars. Without artificial light, it would have been a dark, dank spot for plants, but the tall plants grew abundantly, and the gardener tended to them with equal care given to award-winning roses.

CHAPTER 2

THE CONSTRUCTION OF the new library was finally complete, a large windowless building with air conditioning. It touted a separate reading and periodical room with armchairs and varnished tables, children and teen areas, and an oversized adult section that smelled like plastic. Certain risks were taken by those who wanted to talk, however, by virtue of the multiple arrangements of free-standing shelves, it was possible to remain well hidden from the onslaught of eye-rolling and fingers pressed to lips.

It was 5:00 o'clock the following day when the boy made his way up to the librarian standing behind a tall wooden counter. Behind her was a rolling cart stacked with books waiting to be shelved.

"Do you have *The Bell Jar?*"

"*The Bell Jar?*" she repeated. Her lips hardly moved when she spoke, and he assumed it was because she wanted to make as little a sound come out of her mouth as possible. He nodded.

"We should," she said. "Have you looked on the fiction shelf?"

"No."

She pointed as if giving directions to a motorist. "Walk straight ahead to the P shelf."

"P?" he was confused.

"Silvia Plath," the name fell from her lips with the sarcasm that comes from the pompous ass that she was.

He reviewed the name with indifference.

"She's the author."

"Oh, yeah, I forgot. Silvia Plath," he repeated.

"If you don't mind me asking, aren't you a little young to be reading *The Bell Jar*?"

"*What's it to you?*" But he let her question float around his brain without giving her reason to pout. "Not really, I read all of Plath's work." He smiled and walked away.

To his luck, the book was on a lower shelf, and he didn't have to get one of those small step stools to stand on. He pulled the selection out from between its neighboring books, *The Bell Jar,* a novel by Silvia Plath. He turned it over and began to read the back cover. "I felt very still and very empty, the way the eye of a tornado must feel, moving dully along in the middle of the surrounding hullabaloo." The boy shrugged his shoulders. *Meet me at The Bell Jar.* He wriggled the book back into its place and idly scanned the other books. Then he circumnavigated the shelf. He looked at the wall clock, 5:10. He pulled the book back out and opened it. "This book is a work of fiction. All characters and events are a product of the author's imagination…" A piece of notebook paper was wedged into the binding with the intention of not falling out. *This was my umpteenth visit, and you didn't arrive. If you are reading this note, then at least I know I didn't black-out and expire. Just kidding. I'm recovering under a tree, a gigantic tree, but I would rather be at the movies. I can't come back till Friday, at 5:00 SHARP! Be sure to come alone. Flush this in the toilet after you read it. Adios, amigo.*

The boy shoved the slip of paper into his pocket and put the book back. He thought about the note and then about Silvia Plath and wondered just what the hell is a bell jar.

* * *

HIS SISTER RAN over to him with her hand over her forehead. "I think I'm sick," she said. "Feel my head." He closed the door behind him and followed her brother into the living room. "Really, I feel sick." He sat down on the couch, and she sat next to him. "I can't even finish my ice cream," she moaned. A bowl of chocolate goop was sitting on the coffee table accompanied by several other dirty bowls.

"Probably too much sugar." He leaned back and frowned, showing his unsympathetic side.

His sister burst into a passion of despair, "I am sick, really," and jumping up, she thrust herself into the armchair across the room. "You just don't care!"

"What are you tellin' me for, tell Mom."

"I can't."

"Why not."

"She's not back. Besides, what would she do?"

There were no spare parents around. He knew she was right. "Okay, come here and let me check." But as soon as he said it, the child perked up. "I'm better, I think I feel all better." She sat up and crossed her legs, fitting perfectly in the chair without any room to share. "Seriously, I am." They stared at each other for a moment until the girl said, "What do you want for supper?"

His mind was still wrapped around the thought of what he would have done if she were really sick. Ask the dragon for help?

"What do you want to eat?"

A momentary pause was displaced by "Pizza; we'll have one delivered," he said.

"But we're not supposed to open the door for anyone."

"This is an emergency, we can't starve, can we? With extra cheese."

"And pepperoni?"

"Sure. Go into the kitchen and get the money that's in the jar while I call."

"The bell jar?" she smirked. She was pleased to have answered so cleverly.

"Very funny," he said. *So long as no one knows the secret, they were safe. And now that there was someone else like him, it made things seem better.* The girl returned and handed him the jar. It was light, lighter than the other day. He reached in and counted out the bills. There was enough for pizza and soda. He hoped the dragon wouldn't come around. There was no way they were going to share the pizza.

It was a hot evening, and he wished they lived in a house with air conditioning. The table fan on the floor whirled steadily, scattering dust in the dwindling light beam. The girl went into the kitchen and brought back a glass filled with ice. "Here, want to suck on one?" She shoved her hand into the cup and handed the boy a cube. He didn't really want it but took it anyway. *I can't come back until Friday.* "Two more days for *The Bell Jar*," he thought.

There are all kinds of neighbors, and as much as one would like to choose who they live by, the choice is only as permeant as the residents' decisions to remain. There are the wavers, the reclusive, the snoops, and the "don't give a damn." There are those who are neat, sloppy, finicky, and park it anywhere. Some are renters, freeloaders, guests, or owners. There are the friendly, despised, annoying, or never at home. Gathered into a mass of humanity, these folks go in and out of screen doors, making up what we call "the neighborhood."

The dragon was dormant and sat quietly with his hands pinching his thighs. He stared across the street and watched as the streetlight came on. Same time every night. He was hot and wiped his face with a handkerchief. A car pulled up to the neighboring house. A man too old to be a delivery person got out and started up the walkway.

"Hey, Pizza man!"

"Who me?"

"Yeah, come over and let me pay you." The dragon crammed his hand into his pocket and produced a couple of bills.

"I got a delivery for this house." There was hesitation surrounding the statement.

"That's alright, but I'm gonna pay for it."

The pizza man glanced around for a moment and then walked across a dandelion patched lawn. He stepped up to the porch where the dragon handed him money. Then, he lifted the lid. A heavenly waft of tomato sauce, cheese, and oil was released as he pulled a slice free. "Now, go make the delivery." The dragon smiled and then took a bite.

"Your change."

"Keep it!" A drop of rain tumbled out of the sky. "You better hurry." The dragon lifted his hand and waved it towards the sky. But there was no need for the warning to be sounded; holding his head low, the long-faced man was already scurrying across the yard with his meager tip and a rifled pizza. But all the while, the boy had been watching the transaction through the window. Drops of water were running down the pane. He hadn't been a child for very long, and there was no time to be a youth; all at once, he had been a grown-up. He looked at his sister. She was fiddling with the money. "Put it back in the jar," he said.

"Don't we have to pay the pizza guy?"

"The dragon already did. I saw through the window."

Her face scowled. "Hope he didn't take too many pieces."

Two more days till The Bell Jar.

* * *

THE BOY WOKE up at seven. He wanted to stay in bed a little longer but decided to take a shower before anyone else laid claim to the bathroom. "Coffee," he said. He was going to brew a pot of coffee and have it with his cereal. "No, toast, with coffee and lots of milk and sugar in it." But when he got to the bathroom, he could hear someone rooting around. It was already occupied. It sounded like someone getting up from the floor, and then the noise of something dropping and a voice, "Shit!"

His eyes widened. He held his breath and knew he'd been caught. For some unknown reason, he didn't move.

"Get the hell away from the door, can't anyone have some privacy around here for Christ's sake!" He tiptoed away from the chamber of horrors back to his room. There was no evidence that it was the boy who happened to be standing by the bathroom. He sat on the edge of the bed, thinking how different morning was from night. Suddenly he didn't feel like toast.

"Horseradish. I need something with bite." He wondered what horseradish on a pizza would taste like. The bathroom door opened, a shuffling of bare feet, and then the bedroom door shut. It would be hours until it opened again. And that suited him just fine.

"There's not too much time between night and day, let's go out."

From the backdoor stoop, they could see Mrs. Willy standing in front of the open window drying her hair. "She's naked," the girl said.

The boy looked up. "Nocoo, she's not."

"Almost naked."

"Almost isn't all." He sounded disappointed. They walked around to the front of the house but stopped before they could be seen by the dragon. His porch light was still on, and the geranium plants needed watering. The boy put his fingers to his lips as they stole past his house. There were cars parked along the sidewalk, mostly crappy cars except for a newer silver-colored Lincoln idling on the opposite side of the street with out-of-state plates. "Want to get some horseradish?" The girl's eyes lit up but then dimmed when she realized what he said.

"Nocoo, why would we get that."

"To see who could keep it in their gazzy the longest."

"Seems dexif to me."

"Not any more dexif than eating hot peppers."

"But I don't eat hot peppers."

"I know, that's why horseradish."

She walked a brisk pace ahead and then stopped at the corner. "Where are we going?"

He closed his eyes and sucked in the air. "To the mountains."

She grinned and closed her eyes. "Are they high."

"Very."

"How high?"

"High enough to ski down."

"Are we scared."

"Of course."

"Then maybe we should get some horseradish," she said.

* * *

IT WAS DAY, and the woman failed to appear. Even the dragon remained out of sight. The porch light had been turned off or maybe had burned out sometime during the morning. The girl slipped back from behind the curtain. Snooping had become part of the day's activity. "He's not there," she announced. She tiptoed into the hallway and put her left ear to the door. She put her hand over her right ear and stood very still. "Maybe she's yermied," the girl whispered. The boy frowned and waved his hand for her to move away. But the defiant part of her let him wait for a moment. "Maybe she's yermied," she whispered again and sat in the armchair like a cat.

"Is the paper bag in the bathroom?"

She shrugged. "Maybe someone took it."

"I didn't say it was missing, I just asked if it was in the bathroom."

"I dunno. Should I look?"

There was a quiet silence that gave in to all the answers to their questions. They possessed a secret language, sometimes in their own words, and sometimes a shared understanding. "There are others like us, you know."

She grinned. "How do you know?"

He didn't want to tell her about the two notes. "Just seems logical."

"What if she gets up, and you're not here."

"I didn't say I was going out."

"You are, aren't you?"

"Maybe. Yoyu."

"Maybe or yoyu?"

"Yoyu, but I'll be quick." He wanted to tell her about *The Bell Jar*. It was better if she didn't know."

She got up and walked over to the bathroom, opening the door very slowly, returning after a few minutes. "It's not there. She must have taken the roogs with her in her room."

"Then she won't be up for a while. At least not till after I'm home. Want me to bring back something to eat?" he asked.

"Nocoo, I'm just going to close my eyes and go to the beach."

"Not the mountains?" He liked the mountains.

She shook her head and sighed. "Turn the fan towards me on the way out. You know what it's like at the beach in the summer."

The fan blades hummed, and her hair blew. She was content. He put his key in his front pocket and thought of the woman in the bedroom. She had commandeered his existence, and by doing so, he was destined to fade away. He could conform to what he should be like or try to restore his world. His sister's face looked like a harlequin mask in the greying light. Her chin was raised to the ceiling, and the smile had turned to more of a smirk.

"See you later," he said.

She didn't answer. She was on a raft drifting up and back with the tide.

He opened the front door, but before locking it behind him, he watched the shadows of the retreating sunlight fade.

CHAPTER 3

MRS. POST REMAINED frozen behind the circulation desk. She was listening to a patron for some time who was talking about a novel he wanted the library to order. The librarian had deserted the speaker, only a shapeless mass of thought was steadily keeping track of the conversation. And as a hitchhiker, she joined the dialogue out of necessity. She didn't notice the boy when he entered the double doors. The glass was smudged with fingerprints and needed cleaning. A lousy choice of materials, glass. The wall clock read 4:48, and he sighed with the assumption he was early. He rounded the corner and waded through the stacks of books. P, Pl, Pla, Plat, Plath. His finger ran along the base of each book. PLATH. It was gone. He looked again; PLATH, Silvia Plath, *The Voice of the Poet*, Silvia Plath, *Ariel*. It didn't make sense. It was here two days ago. He walked around the shelf and looked at the clock. 4:55. "Now what?' he thought. The sour-faced librarian was nowhere to be seen and had been replaced by a rounder, more pleasant-looking woman with bobbed white hair and well-manicured nails.

"Looking for this?" The question was solicited by a voice belonging to a wiry boy standing on the far side of the shelf. But as the boy began to speak, he was abruptly interrupted by the newcomer. "Don't look up," he commanded. "Just walk slowly and follow me. But not too close." The speaker was a youth of the same age, a bit shorter, a bit thinner, and walked with a slight limp. They passed a woman sniffling from a cold. Her nose was red, and her eyes were teary. She was scribbling on a pad, taking copious notes from several open books. His eyes caught the woman's, and as if looking in a rear-view mirror, they meet for just a moment. "Bad cold," she said. A handful of tissues were balled up and scattered on the table. She scooped them up and placed them together into one bundle of dirty tissues. "Can you hand me that wastebasket?" she asked.

But he acted as if he didn't hear and moved away from the runny-nosed woman. "Little shit," she grumbled.

"Get it yourself, you got two legs!" cried the limping leader. "They're all the same, think they can boss us kids around. But they're damn mistaken." The boy was impressed with this outburst of defense and suddenly felt as though perhaps this rendezvous would pan out into more than an acquaintance.

They settled at a small round table at the end of the room, where it was occupied by a lone man reading the newspaper attached to a long stick. It looked cumbersome as he tried to maneuver the paper without drawing attention to himself, but it had an uncanny knack of crinkling up as he turned the pages that were spread out in front of him, taking up all the room on the tabletop. "My name's Frito." He put out his hand in a polite gesture.

The boy hesitated; he wasn't sure what to say. There was a long awkward pause after they shook hands. "Frito?" was all that came out of his mouth.

"Frito. Frito Lay."

The boy started to laugh but stopped when the look of bewilderment shook him straight from what he thought was a joke. "You're not kidding, are you?" There was no utterance of laughter. "Your name really is Frito Lay."

The other smiled maniacally. "Just wanted to see if you had a sense of humor. No, that would suck, having a name after a corn chip. My name is Frito, but not Frito Lay. Just Frito."

"Are you Spanish?"

"What if I was."

"Nothing, just thought that you might be, I mean with your name being Frito."

"Does it sound Spanish?"

"No, yes, I don't know." He was confused and shrugged.

"And you, are you Spanish?"

"I don't know, I never asked."

"Asked who."

"Anybody.

"Then maybe you're Japanese."

"Japanese?" He never thought that, but he could be. Weirder things happened. He liked rice. But Spanish people liked rice too.

"What should I call you?"

"Yoshi."

"That sounds Japanese."

"Yes, I know. Like it?"

"Very much."

Frito reached into his pocket and took out a quarter. "Heads you start, tails I start."

"Tails."

"He spun the coin, and it wobbled for a few seconds, however, before it could land, a hand swooped in and took it. Frito frowned. "You're early," he said. The chair legs screeched along the floor as it was pulled out from the table, and a boy sat down. "Yoshi, meet Gustave."

There was a nod between the uninvited and the newbie. "So, you're one of us?"

"He is, I think," explained Frito, "we were just getting to that when you showed up."

"I can leave."

"No, might as well stay. But next time, watch the clock." Tardiness was one of Frito's pet peeves. "I can start off you want." Yoshi nodded with approval. "My father is dead. My mother is also dead. Well, she's not really in the true sense of what would be considered dead. I carry a knife with me and sleep with it under the pillow. That's how I got this." He raised his arm and pulled up his shirtsleeve to expose a white bandage wrapped around his arm just above the elbow. "Nothing serious, just a stupid accident when I was asleep. Now I know to put the knife in a sheath." He rolled his shirtsleeve back and picked up the quarter. The man sitting several yards away had returned the newspaper to the rail and had fallen asleep in the chair. "They make it too comfortable in here," he said, pointing to the sleeping man. "I got a mind to pick his pocket." Yoshi's eyes widened. "Serve him right to sleep in public like that." He twirled the coin, and it spun for several rotations, landing on the table. "Heads, I have to keep going. So, the question you have is what makes us friends. It's simple. We all have assholes for parents. One of them, if not both, are losers."

"Big fat damn losers," added Gustave.

Yoshi looked at Gustave and wondered if he too picked his name. He was a swarthy looking boy with a few light hairs sprouting above his lip. He had sad, dark eyes and was missing a tooth. His shirt was rumpled, and his pants were a bit too short for his height. "Losers," quoted the boy. "I can relate to that."

"When a kid has an asshole for a parent, it's usually for a reason. I mean, a parent just doesn't act like an ass unless there's a catalyst. Usually, it's money. But for us," he looked around and then lowered his voice. "For others like us it's not money, I mean sure money has something to do with it; everyone needs money." He paused and crooked his finger for Yoshi to draw closer. "They're assholes because of one of these reasons, they deal, they buy, they self-medicate. They're on opiates, amphetamine, barbiturates, cocaine, hallucinogens, cannabis, phencyclidine, and prescribed psychoactive drugs. Or they like to drink… all the time. If I left something out, let me know."

Gustave was busy counting on his fingers when he said, "Does cough medicine count?"

"Good one, Gustave!"

"Bottom line, they are selfish sons of bitches that must be dealt with."

Mother must have taken the roogs in her room. The boy heard his sister in his head; her voice louder then Frito's needed to be silenced so he could think. The shape of the man sleeping in the chair was that of a bear. He was a stout fellow with a thick brown beard and a mop for hair. *Maybe he should be pickpocketed,* the boy thought.

"There are many of us," said Gustave. He stuck his tongue in and out of the space where a tooth should be. It was a habit that began to annoy the boy. "Are you in?"

"Am I in?" He felt like he had walked into the middle of a play and not quite sure about the plot. He assumed he knew where it was going but was trying to figure out the direction he was to follow.

They, on the other hand, were looking at him as if they were the audience, and it was time for his soliloquy, but before he took his cue, Gustave interrupted. "It's really quite invigorating once you get to meet more of us. Then you won't feel quite as lonely. And now that it's the beginning of summer, we have so much time."

I like to go to the mountains in the summer, he thought.   Instead, he said, "My mother is a freakshow."

"Good start," said Gustave.

"My Pop, well, he's away."

Both listeners shared the same inaudible signal, a wink.

The man in the chair stirred, and suddenly there was a tap tap tap tap of a pair of heels walking towards them. "Here," whispered Frito. "Take it back to the shelf and only open it right before you put it away." He handed the boy *The Bell Jar*, and before the footsteps could get any closer, he and Gustave pulled their chairs away and rounded out of sight.

"I see you are enjoying that book," said the librarian. She was standing over his chair as if staring into a fishpond. He didn't look up, only slowly pulled the book towards him. "Don't leave on my account. Would you like to check it out?"

"No, thanks, I'm going to put it away."

"Here, let me," she said and reached over to pick it up from the table when he snatched it up. "No, thanks. I just need to finish a paragraph. I'm right at the most exciting part."

Her lips pursed together as if she had tasted something slightly sour. "Suit yourself, just don't reshelve it incorrectly. P-L-A-T-H; she spelled out.

"*A-s-s-h-o-l-e*," he spelled it out in his head before nodding, YES.

He did as instructed; hidden between the pages of the book, the note was waiting for him. *"Nice to meet you. I hope you know how to tend to your garden because it may come in handy sometime soon. Meet me at the Bell Jar next week, Tuesday. I have a dentist appointment Monday. Adios, amigo. Frito. Be sure to flush this in the bathroom right away!"* He tucked the paper in his pocket, stuck the book on the shelf, and looked for the men's room.

* * *

THE BOY STOOD between the door and the mirror. A man was washing his feet in the sink. No apology came from the man, only a question. "Can you give me a hand, I think I'm stuck." The boy looked down at the floor. A pair of dirty socks and sneakers were resting alongside a backpack. There was something quite funny about the situation he found himself in, and without thinking, walked over to the basin. A hand was laid on his shoulder, and the man lifted his leg out. "Thanks, kid, didn't mean to hold you up."

"I had an Uncle this happened to once." He lied.

"Suppose it's a pretty common thing." He pulled out a pack of cigarettes and offered one to the boy. "For your help," he said, shoving the pack towards him.

"No thanks, I don't smoke."

The man squatted down and slipped his wet feet into his socks and shoes. Then he put a cigarette on the side of the basin. "In case you change your mind."

The boy nodded. "See you around," and fumbling with the message in his pocket, he walked into the stall and pulled the lock shut. He thought he heard the bathroom door open and peeked through the space between the stall and the wall. There was no one there. The smell of cleanser suddenly became evident when he lifted the toilet lid. He tossed the paper in. *"For Christ's sake, flush already!"* He took hold of the handle and plunged down. *"Now, get the hell out of that guy's office!"*

* * *

"WHERE'D YOU GET that?" the girl asked.

"From a guy I helped." He let the unlit cigarette hang off his lip as he spoke.

"You look ridiculous," she said. "Aren't you going to light it?"

He knew lots of kids that smoked. "Nope."

"Then what are you going to do with it?"

"Keep it for an emergency. You never can tell when something like this can come in handy."

"You're a jerk, ya know."

"Thank you, I needed reminding of that."

Out of the corner of her eye, she saw the woman's door opening. "Shhh, she's getting up."

An inhuman clearing of the throat entered the room with the mother. Her eyes blinked as she became accustomed to the light. She advanced slowly, still dressed in a hot pink sequenced dress and bare feet. "How long have I been asleep," she asked. She looked around the room as if searching for a place to sit down before settling on the couch. She picked up the cigarette from off the table and searched for the matches.

The boy and the girl looked at each other, waiting for the other to speak.

"Well? And where the hell are the matches?"

"A day," he said.

"Almost a day and the night."

"Which was it a day or a night." Her impatience defined her tone.

"Both," the girl said.

The mother leaned her head back and then tossed the cigarette back on the coffee table. "A day and a half," she muttered and got up to go into the kitchen.

"Must have been some good roog." The girl snickered for a moment but was quickly accosted by her brother with a look of death.

"Shut your gazzy!" he whispered.

The mother came back in and leaned against the chair. "I've got to go out," she said and took a long drink of water. "If Rory comes by, give him the bag."

"Rory?"

"Yes, Rory."

"Rory with the beard?" the girl asked.

"We're just not too sure which is Rory."

She glared. "Yes, tall, dark beard, hat… you've met him a million times."

"Oh, that Rory," the girl nodded.

"If he wants to come in, just say I'm sleeping, and he can't." She placed the grocery bag by the front door and shuffled into her room.

"What about the garden?"

She backed out of the bedroom with her hands on her hips. "What about the garden?"

The sister could see the voices; they were bouncing back and forth like a ping pong ball. Her eyes burned as the volley of words intensified.

"That's what I wanted to know?" He felt emboldened. Maybe because the woman looked so pathetic.

"I heard you, I'm thinking."

All the while, he was smiling in his head. The cigarette, the note, Gustave and Frito; they were all cheering him on. Even the man with the clean feet made him step forward. "Want me to water it?" he asked. "I know how to water plants."

"Alright, that would be good," she decided. "Just be sure to lock the door when you're finished." She walked over and pulled the mirror away from the wall. "The key is here. Just stick it back with tape when you're finished. Now don't bother me, I got stuff to do."

＊ ＊ ＊

SHE HAD KILLED the gardener, but not before killing his dog. It was a lean black dog that did not obey. If it had, it would not have been shot, and then perhaps the entire incident could have been avoided. No one except the woman and the gardener was home when the dog had lunged towards her. He tried to pull the canine back, but its brute strength was greater than he was. The lead slipped from his hand, and the animal tore away free. For several moments it barred its teeth, snapping and growling with ferocious threats. Only the kitchen table stood between the beast and the woman. Several commands were uttered and ignored as it continued to threaten; until, a single shot was fired, a yelp, and it was dead. The room had become quiet. Deadly quiet. Anyone that has loved a dog can understand the emotions of the owner. "You've killed my dog," he said, coming towards her, a little smile lifting by the corners of his mouth. "He had a habit of digging. Did you know that? He liked to dig holes?" The gardener took several steps forward, and she took several steps back. He had a knife in his hand. She didn't see him pick it up, but he must have seen the bread knife in the dish tray.

"Take your damn dog and get the hell out of my house." Her gun remained by her side; her finger poised on the trigger.

"Here, boy, here, come on, boy." The man pointed with the knife. "He can't hear me," he said. "Did I tell you that I raised him from a pup?" He was sweating now and wiped his forehead on his shirt sleeve.

"If you come any closer, I'll have to shoot." And then, she did.

A felon and a dog and the words of a mother. The detective agreed; she had no other choice but to defend herself. He had become enraged. "Desperate" was the word used in the newspaper. But even if you're acquitted of murder, there is always a stigma attached. There are those who place judgment upon your character, forever wary, critical, and always disapproving. The dragon didn't seem to care, and so they trusted him, not as a friend but as a silent partner.

But now it was up to the mother to do the gardening, a chore that at first had become burdensome. But after the crop was harvested and she no longer had to share in the profit, she was happy. It was easy to work, the plants grew effortlessly, tall and leafy, thick with buds and knots of flowers.

She had no love for plants and thought herself a hack when it came to growing flowers, yet the present rate of growth by these weeds were more than prolific; it had become damn profitable. Still, there was time between the new shoots and the drying of the old leaves where she still had to rely on others.

"How come we always have to go to the store?"

"You know why."

"But it was such a long time ago."

"I guess not long enough."

"But people still stare at us," she moaned.

He didn't answer and took the list. "Well, just ignore them."

She made a face. "But I can hear what they say even when they're whispering. Dog killer."

"That dog sucked anyway. It deserved what it got. I hated that dog."

"And Milo, you hated him too."

"Not anymore, he's dead."

"Well, take the key, it's your turn," he handed it to the girl with infinite confidence. "Here, Saachi, take it."

"What did you call me?'

"It's an Indian name, I think it means truth." He shrugged. "Like it?"

"I guess it's okay. And what should I call you? Shithead."

"If you want. I don't really care." She looked at him with a sarcastic expression and snatched the key. "Yoshi, it's what you can call me."

"Saachi and Yoshi, okay."

"What should we call her?" she giggled with secret ideas.

"Henrietta."

It was a short walk to the grocery store. The sister had enough money and enough attitude to get the items on the list. The brother watched from the window until she was out of sight. *Is there something wrong? No. Then water the plants. Get the key stupid; you know where it is, don't you.* The mirror pulled away from the wall as he slipped his hand behind; the key easily came free. The hallway appeared longer and darker, and he suddenly felt nervous. He stood before the padlock, and his hands began to tremble as he poked the key into the lock when there came a rap rap rap on the back door. His heart jumped, and he stood perfectly still. Rap Rap Rap. No one came around by way of the back door, they always walked up the front steps. He pulled the key from the padlock and walked into the kitchen. "Who's there?"

"Open the damn door, it's me, Rory."

The boy realized he felt no sense of danger. He fumbled with the door, and it sighed as it was pushed open. The man standing before him now seemed so much taller than when he was on the step. He was standing very straight, like a soldier. "What took you?"

"I was in the bathroom." He lied.

"Is your mother home?" he asked, stepping into the room further than the boy intended. He glanced around, yet there showed no movement of anyone else being home.

"She's asleep." He lied.

"I have something she may want. It was left with me." He handed the boy a wrapped package.

"Where's your sister?"

"She went to the store."

"Alone?" The bearded man acted concerned.

The boy nodded.

"Be sure to give it to your mother." The tobler had stationed himself between the door frame with the tip of his head almost touching the top. He looked around and then asked. "The bag?"

The boy set the package on the table and turned into the living room. For a split second, he wondered what would happen if Rory followed him, but he didn't. "Here," he said, returning with the sack.

"Thanks, kid." He smiled and then turned to leave when he stopped. "Do you like cats?"

"Cats, I suppose."

"I saw some kittens outside, and if you want, I'm sure you can have one."

The boy thought for a moment and then remembered the incident with the black dog. "I better not. Thanks anyway."

"Summertime, long days, aren't they kid?"

The boy stood on the back stoop and wanted to say something but had a loss for words. He closed the door and suddenly felt curiously different. He turned to the kitchen drawer and pulled out the scissors. He snipped the twine and removed the wrapping paper. It was a book. He opened the pages and leafed through. There were a series of names, a few starred, and a couple had strikes drawn through with a red pen. Manny Milo. It had been crossed out. He didn't see the dog's name. It didn't seem that the list could then be complete. *I hated that dog, it deserved what it got.*

* * *

THE STRANGE PLANTS were basking under the fluorescent lights more like a science experiment than a garden. Each plant required distilled water sprinkled across the light loam of sturdy rows. He reached out with one hand and picked a leaf, wondering what she would say if she saw him. Then he walked to the end of the row and plucked another. The room felt clammy and cold, and he shivered. He ducked behind a fence of weeds growing in what looked like small coffins and smelling faintly like a wet meadow of manure. He had a clear shot of the door. It was a wonderful room to play hide and seek in. He stood up and placed the watering can back in the plastic bin. He could hear his sister rumbling around in the refrigerator. It wasn't a very pretty garden, for that matter it was ugly. It would be so much nicer if they were roses.

CHAPTER 4

O N THE MORNING of the meeting, the rain had stopped. It had been pouring all night; the mother cat had carried her kittens beneath the dragon's house. She found a dry spot where she deposited the three in a box, and all night long, they cried. No one heard their complaints except Henrietta. "If I find those damn cats, I'll make stew!" However, no one seemed alarmed by the idle threats since the woman never cooked.

The dragon walked up and down the sidewalk, which was making it difficult to go outside. Saachi tossed the curtain aside. "I'm going out when he goes inside. Until then, I'll be in my room. I want pizza for supper and make it all cheese this time."

"I'm going out too," Yoshi said.

"What about her?"

"What about her?"

"Did she get the bag back? Cause if she got the bag back, then she won't be up for days."

I don't know," he said. "But she's got to get up soon for the garden. It's like a jungle in there, want'a see?"

She shook her head, no. "If she's yarmied, then the garden will have to wait. Besides, it's just a bunch of stupid weeds."

They stood there in the middle of the room for a moment. Whenever he left her alone, a feeling of concern was ignited. "The dragon isn't so bad."

She frowned.

"No, really. I don't think he's such a bad guy. Kind of weird looking."

"Why, because he shaves his head except for one little grey ponytail sticking up?"

The boy shrugged. "No, it's because he wears that robe and pajama pants."

"I think we should visit him," her thought alighted as she spoke aloud.

"I gotta go."

"Can I come?" But in the time it took for him to renege, she had already declined. "Never mind, I don't want to go with you."

She followed him to the door. "See you later, with a pizza."

"With a cheese pizza. I wonder how many more of us are out there living on pizza?" She shut the door, and he heard it lock.

* * *

IT TOOK A moment for the meaning of her suggestion to take effect. *We should visit him sometime.* The mother cat scampered by, and he hoped she had moved her kittens. He could crawl under the house to check, but he was in a hurry. He wanted to get to the library before Frito. The dragon was sitting on his porch and waved. He waved back meekly and hurried along before the man called him up. He didn't want to talk, not now. A woman with a baby stroller saw him approaching and crossed the street. *Murderer's children.* "She wasn't charged," he shouted. The woman scowled and pushed the stroller faster. He could hear the baby laughing. It sounded like the baby had shouted, but it was too little. Babies don't talk. It was that woman. *They never forget.*

In the library, a few patrons were waiting in a queue to check out their books. The boy followed his usual path along the strip of carpet towards fiction. An elderly woman was wandering the shelves as if on a pilgrimage. Every now and again, she would stop and push a book that appeared out of place, so it was evenly in line one beside the other. Then she would continue to walk until she spotted another out of place and repeated the pattern. When the "Ps" were finalized, she moved along to another shelf. Yoshi pulled Silvia Plath from the shelf. His eyes took in everything around him before he opened to the middle of the book and slipped in the two leaves from the garden. He returned the book to the shelf and positioned himself at a table next to a shaded window. Beyond the glass, there was a footpath that led to the meditation garden with benches and a bronze statue of Charles Burnings II, a prominent philanthropist and bibliophile. A small plaque had been erected, giving thanks for his Dedication as a Friend of the Library. "*If he was so great why didn't they put him in the front of the building,*" Yoshi thought.

He breathed in the familiar smell of new and old books. It was an unchanging smell. There was nowhere else he remembered having such a smell except the library. He sat silently and anticipated his meeting when, after an unknown amount of time, there exclaimed, "Good one!" It was Frito. He held the book and two leaves in his hand. "You've passed the first test!" he exclaimed.

"Test?"

"Yes, you are definitely one of us. You've proven it with these," he laughed and handed the crumpled leaves back to Yoshi.

"You can have them."

"No, thanks, keep 'em yourself." He sat down and drummed the table. "There's some others you need to meet."

The boy smiled. "Okay, when?"

"Now, right now."

"Now?" he was confused.

"Follow me, they're waiting."

"Where?"

"In the bathroom," and moving away from the table, he began to limp quickly in the direction of the Men's Room.

"*In his office?*" Yoshi followed, but when he opened the door, Frito was not there. Only two others, one was sitting on the side of the basin and the other leaning against a closed stall. The man with the clean feet was not inside.

"Frito said to give you this." A heavy-set boy handed him *The Bell Jar*. He opened to the inside page and pulled out a note. *Now there are four, see you in 2 days. Adios amigo, you know the drill...flush it!*

"Frito says you're one of us."

The boy nodded.

"I'm Hawk, and this is Kojo." A tall, lean boy offered a reserved smile.

"I'm Yoshi."

"You live next to the dragon," Kojo said. The boy looked suspiciously uneasy with this information. "Everyone like us knows the dragon. And then there's Rory. Sometimes you get a bag delivered to your house, and sometimes you deliver it back."

"I thought…"

He was interrupted, "You thought your mother, Henrietta, was the only one. It doesn't work that way." Hawk grinned. "Don't worry, we have the same secret. In fact, we're more alike than you can ever imagine."

Hawk went over to the basin and started to wash his hands. "Shhh, someone is coming, get in the stall!" Yoshi followed the command and shut the door, Kojo slipped into the adjacent one, and while the faucet water was running the door opened and closed. "Coast is clear." He pulled several paper towels free. "There is one more test you have to perform," said Hawk. "We've all done it. But for you, it might be a little more difficult."

"We're a little more lucky, or not lucky, depending on your point of view. To really rid yourself of your problem, you have to eliminate it." It occurred to Yoshi that Kojo was talking from recent experience.

"Think of it as a cleansing," Hawk said. The spiky-haired boy began to tip back and forth on his heels.

"Why will my test be more difficult than both of yours?"

Kojo placed his hand on the boy's shoulder. "Because afterward, you'll have more responsibility. You'll have us of course." The shortlist seemed to satisfy all that needed to be explained. "You shouldn't have too much trouble."

"Too much trouble?"

"Keeping it a secret."

"We're all going to be good friends, and many more of us too. We've all been in your shoes, and you can't believe how invigorating it becomes once you're done," Hawk added. He looked down at his watch. "We gotta go! Say in two days we can meet again. Say noontime. Give what we said some thought." The bathroom door opened with the smell of new books. "Don't forget to flush."

Yoshi put his hand in his pocket and rustled the note. *The Bell Jar* felt heavy in his hand. He walked into the stall and tossed the book into the toilet. It was too big to surrender itself to the bowl and appeared to have been levitated rather than floating. A sudden sensation of panic rose, and he pulled the novel from the water and frantically began to dry the plastic cover on his shirt. Only a few pages appeared to be wet. The toilet was flushed, and he watched the note get sucked down the drain. "I saved you from drowning, Silvia Plath."

Sorry, I can't do the same, she said.

CHAPTER 5

HOW LONG HAS it been since she combed her hair? The boy looked at his sister. He hadn't noticed it before today. There was something wild about her, and then it occurred to him that they were more like wild animals than domesticated pets. *There are others like us.* He would have to tell her about the others. She had a right to know. And the dragon, would he have to know too? That question didn't need to be settled right away. "Where's the bag?"

"She must have gotten it. I heard her get up, but I didn't come out of my room. I think I heard the front door open and close."

"Are there any paper bags left in the kitchen?"

"I didn't think of that. Yeah, it must have been a tobler."

The boy thought for a minute. "Did you hear any names?"

She seemed annoyed. "I don't know, I was half asleep." She lied.

"You don't know, or you didn't hear?" He pressed her.

"Someone she called 'honey.'"

He made a face.

"There was more than one person, honey and Longo. Then she said, 'good work Longo.' I think they were women."

Yoshi got up and walked into his room, returning with the black book. He thumbed through the list, which had been alphabetically indexed. "She's here. Margaret Longo, but no honey." He smiled. He handed the book to his sister. The tobler left it for Henrietta."

"What are these little stars?"

He shrugged.

"And the ones crossed out?"

It seemed obvious to him. "It's a list of toblers, the ones crossed out are gone." He made a gesture with his hand as if slitting his throat.

Her finger was drawn up and down the page. "Milo!" He's here!" She continued to look. "But not the dog." She seemed disappointed.

"And now you've crossed over the boundary."

"What the hell are you talking about?"

"Freedom Saachi, freedom.

* * *

THE FIRST TRIP to the dragon's house was to escape. Henrietta was moving furniture out to make room for the garden, so they walked next-door to the dragon. He was asleep on the porch, and the brother and sister were pelted by loud snores of indifferences running out of his nose. "What's that?" the sister asked. It was an upside-down broom. "Not that," she whispered. "That."

"A chicken foot."

"For soup?"

"Maybe."

She wriggled her nose with disgust.

The second trip to the dragon house was to escape. Henrietta was smoking and fell asleep, so they walked next door to the dragon while the smoke cleared. It wasn't much of a fire, only a cushion. He wasn't asleep on the porch. The boy and the girl sat on an old wooden swing while the dragon sat on a porch chair with a cat on his lap. A large black and white cat named Mrs. Scott. "What's that?' the sister asked.

"A bell."

"Why is it wearing a bell?"

"So she doesn't eat the birds."

"You like birds?" the boy asked.

"Yes, they can be very delicious."

That was the first time the boy and the girl spoke to the dragon. There was a knock on the door several days later. A minute lapsed when there was a louder rap rap rap. "Answer the damn door and see what they want!"

"It's the guy from next door. Should I open it?" The girl was peeking through the peephole.

"Tell him no one is home!" the mother shouted.

"No one's home!" This was the second time they spoke to him. "I think he left something." She watched as he went down the steps and back to his house. As soon as he was out of sight, the boy edged the door open and brought the tin inside. "It's a box."

"A what?"

"A box made out of metal." He shook it.

"Bring it," the mother said.

"Let me carry it!" squealed the girl, and she pulled it away. The mother was lying in bed; her robe was stretched across the chair with an electric fan aimed directly at her.

"Who did you say it was from?"

"That guy, you know who always sits on his porch."

She nodded. "Hand me a cigarette. And the matches." The boy and the girl looked at each other with wide eyes. "Don't worry, I won't burn the house down." They were.

"Let's open it," suggested the boy.

"Who, you and the mouse in your pocket?" The girl laughed. The lid was stubborn but was finally pried open. A small leather pouch sitting on a bed of straw emanated a strong odor.

"It smells kind of like perfume."

"More like shit," the woman said and dropped the pouch back.

"What's it for?"

"Hell if I know. He made a mistake. Must be for a different house. Take it back."

"Take it back?" the brother asked.

"What are you a parrot. Take the damn thing back."

Fearful indecision was cluttering his mind. "Now?"

"Yes, right now, I don't want that thing in the house," she demanded.

"But it was a present," the sister said.

"If you two don't take this thing out of my room, I will make you eat it for dinner!" They thought she was kidding, but there was nothing on her face to indicate such a notion. The afternoon had come to an end. It was clear that the gift would be returned right away. There was nothing further for them to do but to simply wait until the dragon was inside and put the tin by the doormat when he was asleep.

But, unbeknownst to the mother, it was returned empty except for a handwritten note that read, "thanks."

* * *

FOUR DAYS A week, the street-sleeper goes into his office. He freshens up and then returns to sit in his regular chair by the periodicals, reads for a few hours, saunters into the meditation garden if the weather permits for a smoke, and then back into the office until he is ready to leave. The other three days of the week are spent riding the transit system. A tall, slim built man, between the age of 40 or 45 with greying hair and a scrubby silver peppered beard. He has a snake on his arm that starts at the wrist and winds up beneath his shirt sleeve and tips its tongue at the nape of the neck. Usually, when he arrives at the office, there isn't anyone inside, but this Tuesday, the boy was there waiting.

"I brought you this; my Uncle said it was the best." He lied.

The man took the bar of soap and put it to his nose.

"I can get more if you want."

He tossed it into his bag and nodded. "An excellent grade of soap, thank you." He turned to his bag and fumbled inside. "Cigarette?"

He shook his head no. "My name is Yoshi."

"Sikes."

"You like books?"

"I like libraries," he grinned. "And books. They keep me company when it's cold and when it's not cold." The boy didn't say anything and stood for a few moments awkwardly watching as a half-eaten sandwich was unwrapped from a grease-stained newspaper. "Want some?" The boy shook his head.

"I guess I'll get going and let you eat. I can see you're busy." He smiled.

"Maybe just a little; but stop by anytime and thanks for the soap." He leaned against the wall behind the door and began to eat his sandwich. The light flickered, and for a second, the bathroom went dark. "I need to tell them about the wiring," he mumbled. He glanced up and saw that the boy was gone. Only a note had been left by the sink. *I live nearby if you need something to eat. Yoshi.* He finished his sandwich and threw away the paper. He stretched, picked up his backpack, and walked into the stall. "Curious little kid," he thought. He would keep the boy in his pocket. Some days meals are harder to come by than others.

* * *

HENRIETTA LOOKED IN the bag and approved. "What the hell happened to your eye?" It was a big fish-eye, bloated around the edge. "Looks like it hurts."

The woman winced with the mention of the eye. "It does."

"See anybody about it."

"No."

"Maybe you should."

"So, do you want the shit or not?" she changed the subject.

"Yea, just do me a favor. Don't come around anymore when my kids are here."

"When the hell is that?"

She handed Longo the money and crumpled the paper bag so it would stay closed. "Want a cup of coffee?"

"Coffee? I don't drink coffee anymore; it gives me the jitters." The redhead walked over to the back door and started for the knob.

"I'll call when I need you then," Henrietta said. She leaned over the table as though fastened to the seat and pulled a cigarette from the pack. One was already burning in the ashtray.

The redhead was a tired-looking woman without any reason to hurry, but she did. "You'll always need me," she remarked. She winked her good eye and then wriggled her skirt down along her hips and yanked her blouse up above her cleavage. "Things always seem to be sagging."

There was a closing of the door. The woman sat for a few moments, content with the afternoon. She opened the bag and grinned. A stack of mail had been piling up, all junk except for a check from the government. She wasn't in the mood to go to the bank. All those damn accusatory faces. Especially that bitchy, smartass teller. She'd send the boy or the girl, she decided. They were old enough to go. All they needed was an endorsed check and the account number. She took a drag on the cigarette and snuffed the butt of the other one out. She tore open the letter and pulled the check out from the envelope. "I need one of you!" she screamed. She flipped the check over and signed her name. A minute passed, and the cigarette burned freely in the overfilled ashtray. She took a drag of the butt and tapped her foot. "I need one of you right now! Now, now, now, damn it! NOW!"

"I was in the bathroom!"

"Where's your brother?"

She shrugged.

"Don't give me that mopey "I don't know" look. I asked you a question."

"Honest, I think maybe asleep." She lied.

"At this hour?"

She shrugged.

"Pour me a cup of coffee." The girl reached for the cup. "No, never mind. I need you to go to the bank."

"Bank?"

"Yes, the bank. Is there a problem?"

She nodded, no. She lied. She hated the teller.

"Here, cash this. If they give you any shit, tell them your mother will change banks." She handed the girl the check. "And don't lose it!"

"I won't." There was something very compelling about being in charge of so much money. She couldn't wait to tell the boy. But her sudden elation was squashed by the thought of walking into town.

"Get going, it doesn't stay open all night. And when you get home, put the money in the jar. Order a pizza if you want or Chinese."

The girl felt her way around the darkness of Henriette's words. She wondered if she could catch what her mother had. He had told her, *'There are others like us.'* Was that supposed to be a good thing? She folded the check and put it in a small change purse. Then she put the leather amulet around her neck and tucked it beneath her shirt, making a little bulge. *No one will give me any shit now,* she thought. A cheese pizza with sausage would be good just as long as the dragon doesn't take a piece. Yoshi will be pleased.

* * *

THE TELLER LOOKED at the check and at the endorsed name. *From the account of the murderess.* It was a man teller. She had never seen a man behind the bank window before. He had a small but bushy mustache and thick-rimmed glasses. He pecked the amount into the register. "Will twenties be alright for your *murderess mother*? The girl stood on her tiptoes and nodded, "yes." She read his name tag, Francis Collins, as he counted out the bills and a few coins. "Should I put this in an envelope?" She hadn't planned her exit from the bank very well. All the money wouldn't fit into the small change purse. She nodded, "yes." "There you go, young lady" He handed her a small white envelope. "If there's nothing else I can do for you, have a nice day."

The girl stepped aside and let the next customer up to the teller's window. *The murder's child is very nice but has a rather odd smell.* But the response from the listener got muffled in the order of her brain. It was working frantically to decide where to hide the envelope. The money was a responsibility she had to take seriously. When no one was looking, she knelt down and pushed it into her sock. "There," she decided, "not bad for a murderer's daughter." She pulled the amulet up from her shirt and smelled it. "I knew it would bring me good luck," and quickly slipped it back down. She turned her face to a woman that happened to be looking her way and stuck her tongue out before pulling open the heavy door and skipping out.

It was a very nice day for a walk, everything seems nicer when you have money. The girl paid no attention to the couple at the corner waiting to cross the street. They were a pair of embittered old fools that snapped at each other like barracudas. She didn't even care if they said she was from the "killing house." Right now, nothing was going to bother her. When she got to the dragon's, she stood on the sidewalk to see if he was on the porch. He was. The black and white cat was not on his lap, and instead, he was peeling a lemon. She went to the bottom step of the porch and waited. He didn't see her. He had a paring knife and was meticulously removing the outer skin. A long single peel was uncoiling and dangling by his foot. When the lemon had been freed from its rind, he bit into the fruit, offering no indication it was tart.

"Isn't that sour?" she asked. She had edged up the steps and was standing beside him, watching his lips. But never once did they pucker. Instead, he smacked them with satisfaction.

He turned his face towards her. "Makes you know that you're alive." She looked perplexed. "Lemons are the soul of fruit. But I don't think you want to eat a lemon." He put his hand into his pocket and pulled out licorice. She grinned and took it. Then she backed away and sat on the top step. He picked up another lemon from a bowl beside his chair. "Do you know what I'm going to do with this lemon?" he asked.

"Eat it?"

"No," he said, and holding it between his thumb and fingers, he showed it to her. "I am going to give it to you for protection. Before you go to bed, put some slices of this lemon and a pinch of salt together in a bowl and slide it under your bed. It will act like a sponge and absorb the negative energy while you sleep." She turned and looked towards her house. The envelope in her sock was irritating her skin, and she wanted to remove it. Her eyes fell to the window where she thought she saw the boy looking out from behind the curtain. "After three days, get rid of the salt and lemon by burying it away from the house. Do you understand?"

"Three days." She repeated his words.

"Three," and holding up his fingers, he fluttered them. He had a large hand and very neat fingernails, as though he spent time having them manicured. "Here."

She took the lemon as a sign that her stay may be over. "Thanks for the candy."

The black and white cat had jumped up and now was taking up all his attention. A car drove by clanking and cluttering with a broken muffler. He closed his eyes, tuning out all noises. "In three days," said the girl. He didn't hear her.

∗ ∗ ∗

HE NEVER COULD subject himself to pain until he met Frito. "If you don't let us, then Gustav will have to hit you with the stick even harder." He looked down at the floor and contemplated being smashed with a stick.

"He gets no joy from doing it," Kojo explained. "It's just that since he found the stick, he gets to."

That seemed fair, thought the boy.

"So, what will it be? We really need to get on with it."

"I guess the belt, but do it where no one will see," he said.

"We each get a turn; it will be fast."

"It's only a belt," said Hawk. Gustav set the stick aside while Frito removed his belt.

The boy closed his eyes and held fast to the basin. Three lashes behind the legs and one on his back. He wondered which asshole that was. When it was over, he ran over to the stall and vomited.

"Congratulations, you're one of us."

"I think I hate you," said the boy. He walked out of the stall sickened by the bitter treatment they had given him. He groped for some rational, his hands shaking, and his eyes blurry. He turned on the water and drank from the faucet.

"It'll only sting for a little while," explained Kojo. "Just don't take a hot shower tonight."

He tried to rub his leg, but it hurt too much to touch. A lot of shit happened in his life, but he had never been whipped.

"It may hurt now, but you'll find out in a few hours it'll be gone." Frito was feeling philosophical. "We stimulated pain by striking you with the belt. When we stopped, so did your pain."

"Almost," the boy said.

"But for the most part, by eliminating the pain, you immediately feel better."

Such illogic was logical. "Stay here for a few minutes, you look pretty bad."

"Thanks," he said. He pulled a few paper towels from the dispenser and soaked them in water. The paper was rough, but the water felt good on his face.

"Go to *The Bell Jar* before you leave, brother."

He kept the towel on his face until each boy had left. He had always wanted a brother, and now he had four. Frito, Gustav, Kojo, Hawk, and then others. *There are others out there like us.* If there are more, we'll have to find a new meeting place other than the library bathroom, he thought.

CHAPTER 6

SIKES SAT ON the department store bed. He lay down and put his hands behind his head. "This is the kind of bed I could get used to." It had been quite a long time since he remembered lying on a mattress, and when the salesman came over, he closed his eyes.

"May I help you, Sir?"

He opened one eye and then the other. "Just testing it out."

The salesman stood vigil over the customer as if he were going to steal the merchandise. "Have you got one of a better quality, maybe a little firmer. This one feels a little soft." He rolled off the bed and picked up his backpack. Sikes was a lanky man, well over six feet, and towered over the squat salesman with flat feet. He hated this job, but jobs were hard to come by.

"We have a better line of mattresses over here," he said and reluctantly gestured the disheveled customer to follow. "This is the Queen Anne line of mattresses. Would you like to try?"

"Is it firm?"

"I believe it will be to your liking."

"Oh, yeah, you know your line of business," Sikes said and rolled from side to side. A family of four were roaming the rows wearing their most disgusted look of disapproval as they approached. "Just testing it out." He tapped the side of the bed, "Here, there's plenty of room," but when the little girl started to climb up, the mother pulled her back in horror, chastising the child for her friendliness.

"It is a good mattress," the salesman reaffirmed with his eye on the family who seemed to be interested in twin beds.

"Let me have your card," said Sikes. He sat up and leaned against the headrail. "I'm going to be coming into some money pretty soon."

The salesman opened his wallet and offered a card. *Wendel Wilkes*

"Well, Mr. Wilkes, it's been a pleasure making your acquaintance. Maybe we could have a drink sometime." He turned his feet to the floor and stretched. He dropped the card into his shirt pocket, but before strutting off, he brushed the bottom of the bed with his hand. "Underbridge dust can be a real chore to keep things clean once it gets on your shoes." Wilkes followed the light footprints as they traveled across the carpet to the elevator, where he watched the dusty man get in. "See you, Wendel," he shouted. There was a half-hearted wave from the salesman as the door closed. Pinched by envy the bored salesman trundled off into the sea of mattresses and box-springs. He straightened his bowtie, and with a stroke of his comb smoothed his hair. He looked at his watch and frowned, not at the time but at the thought of bologna sandwich again. Tomorrow he would be different, he decided. Tomorrow he would bring soup.

⋆ ⋆ ⋆

"SHE'S IN HER bedroom with three other gryphons."

"Did you see them go in?" the boy asked. He sat down without leaning back in the chair.

"I answered the door."

"How do you know they were gryphons*?*"

"Because none of them wanted any of the pizza," she said.

He stood up and pulled free a piece of the leftover pie and put it on a napkin. "Want some soda?" Two glasses were taken out of the sink and rinsed before going into the freezer. "There isn't any ice."

"And no soda either."

"I thought you were going to the store." His disappointment was tempered by the satisfaction of cold pizza.

"She sent me to the bank. Look in the jar, there's money."

He turned but didn't get up. "You went?"

"It was easy, all she did was write her name on the back, and the teller handed over the cash."

He continued chewing. Somehow he felt like something was missing. "Just like that?"

"Yep." The girl looked over her shoulder and made a sign of four fingers walking across the table. "I think they're coming out," she whispered, her voice barely audible.

Their mother had tried to maintain her youth; however, her current habits far outweighed her ambitions. She leaned back and held herself up against the doorframe. "They're just leaving," she said to the children. A young man with yellow teeth and yellow hair kissed Henrietta on the cheek as he squeezed past her. The red-headed woman and a dumpy blonde companion followed behind. "Want your shit?"

"What shit?" asked the blonde.

"Never mind, then." The door closed, and Henrietta sighed at first with contentment and then with contempt. "This place is a pigsty." Her toe was bleeding, and she bent over to wipe the blood from her foot with a dishtowel. "I cut myself, that's all. Just watch where you walk in the bathroom, there still might be some glass. I gotta get a cigarette," she said and turned back into her bedroom.

They listened as she rummaged around until it grew quiet again.

"Know what?" the boy asked.

"What?"

"She can rot in that room for all I care." His heart had hardened against her. He felt a kind of fluttering in his chest as one who loses something important. The girl pulled off a piece of pizza and began to pick the cheese off the top. "It's amazing the stuff you can come up with over cold pizza," he said. Suddenly there was no more pain. His legs were okay, and his back only felt a tinge different. "Want some water?" She nodded yes, but what her mouth really wished for was soda. "There's a piece of tomato still on your gazzy." He handed her a napkin, and she wiped it clean. "There's one piece left, want to split it?"

They ate in silence, everything looked the same; the open pizza box, the dirty dishes, cereal boxes, and soda cans. They had no idea when Henrietta would get up. "We can spy on the dragon," the girl said and pulled her chair away from the table. She crooked her finger for the boy to follow, and they slipped behind the curtains. "I don't see him."

The grey sky fell over the house. Twilight always increased the feeling of dread, but by nighttime, the darkness had swallowed all the fear. "There he is."

He ascended the stairs with the black and white cat slinking behind. "I think he's carrying something. Did you know that werewolves and vampires were cousins?" Her nose pressed lightly against the window.

"I don't think it's a wolf he's got. It's a kitten."

"Are you sure?"

"No. Look, he's going inside."

Disappointment fell over the girl. "We can see him tomorrow," she said. She sat on the floor behind the curtain, her head leaning against the wall. "I think I'll stooky for a while. If she comes out, don't tell her where I am."

The boy pulled the drapes apart and walked over to the refrigerator. He looked in and wondered what he would give Sikes if the man happened to come by. He shook the container of milk and decided that there would be enough to share. Cereal was good any time of the day. A whispering argument was stirring around in his head. He couldn't really tell what it was about and told himself he needed quiet. It stopped. "I'm going to bed." He waited for a moment.

The girl didn't stir.

He left the lamplight on and trundled off to his room. "Goodnight."

A faint reply circled the room like a wisp of air but fell short of reaching him as the door shut behind him.

"We don't need her anymore................."

* * *

THE DRAGON SLEPT well on his palm fiber sleeping-pallet. An animal hide was spread on the floor beneath it. It was a stark bedroom consisting of a few sticks of furniture: a wooden table, chair, and low dresser. Upon entering these quarters, one would assume he was a simple man; however, the rest of the house contradicted this notion. Inside the kitchen, a cooking pot on the stove held the remains of boiled plantains. But what was most striking about the room was the wall behind the stove, an elaborate fresco of a horse. An oblong table was set with calabash utensils on top of a red and white checkered tablecloth. Neat and orderly, a cupboard and shelves were piled with tin goods and crockery, none of which matched. An antique buffet and mirror were pushed against the dining room wall. No other furniture adorned the room except a wire rack of fine French wines and bottles of unknown contents. The square-shaped living room housed a stone fireplace that occupied one entire wall. A slightly elevated table with earthen jugs of seed pods and oils was surrounded by floor cushions sewn from a thick, hardy material with an exotic smell. The interior walls were muted and colorless, almost primitive in appearance. This was the home of the dragon, a man that did not like waste, especially words. Three individual glass tanks, two terrariums, and a fish tank aligned the entire back wall of a library. Constructed on three walls were shelves of books, and except for the two glass tanks, there were no other furnishings.

The first time she viewed the floating world, she tapped the wall of the tank. It was just a light tap, one that the fish ignored. "It's not accustomed to others," the dragon said. She watched as the fish swam behind an undulating fringe of reeds before escaping into a cave of rainbow-colored coral.

"Does it have a name?"

"No."

The girl waited for a few minutes, but it did not show itself. "What's in here?" she pointed.

"Frogs."

She made a scowl until she walked over and peered cautiously into the glass. "That's a frog?"

"Pretty little fellow, isn't he."

"I've never seen a yellow frog, or one so small."

"And very picky eaters." He pointed to a smaller tank of anthropoids. A tiny look of revulsion appeared on her face. He could tell that she had had enough. "Perhaps I should give you those lemons," he said.

* * *

"FROGS?" THE BOY seemed interested.

"And bugs, and fish too. He's very interesting. And books, tons of books."

"What kind of books?"

"I don't know, just books."

"Did you see *The Bell Jar*?"

"I said books, not jars."

Sometimes the girl was too dense. "The book, *The Bell Jar*, was it on the shelf."

She shrugged. "I got more lemons." She was hiding them in her room. "Is she home?"

"Maybe, but you gotta be careful when you go into the bathroom. I think I got a piece of glass in my foot."

"How do you know?"

"It feels like a bee sting, but I can't see it."

"Did you tell Henrietta?"

"Not when she's yarmied. Remember the last time. Face it, we can't trust her; she's dactie."

"Dactie." The girl repeated the word. The space had gotten wider now between herself and Henrietta. "Go to the dragon, he can look at your foot." It was a splendid idea, and his eyes glowed with favor until he fell into dubious thoughts.

"Do you think he would?"

Of all things that could provoke a superior smile, it is when in the presence of doubt. "Come on, I'll show you," she said and tossed the boy his socks and sneakers. But after putting on them on, he reverted from his usual quick steps to taking on very gentle movements as if he were going to step on ice. "This wouldn't have happened if she wasn't so dactie," he protested.

"Come on!" She waited impatiently with the door open, but as she watched the boy, there was a sorrow about him that she never wanted to notice. "Here, let me help you," she said. She put her arm around his shoulder, and he leaned in. "Too bad about your foot." She escorted him down the steps and onto the grass. The dragon was on the porch, and they saw him. Without any need to ask, he got up from his chair and stood at the top of the porch as the pair approached with friendly innocence. He turned to the front door and waited. "It's his foot, he got glass in it." The dragon remained stone-faced, and they followed him into the house. There was a smell in the air coming from the kitchen. It was more than hovering; it was an odor that once caught in your nostrils, it remains.

"Take off your shoe," he said. "I'll be right back." Through an open door, Yoshi could see the library. There was something decidedly inviting about the room, perhaps it was the sunlight spilling onto the floor.

The dragon returned, carrying a large pot with what smelled like white vinegar. "This is good for removing sea urchin spines too," he said. "Sit here," he motioned to a three-legged stool. "Soak your foot; I'll be back."

The girl folded herself into a floor cushion. "I'll be at the beach if you need me," she said and closed her eyes.

The boy had time to think as the skin began to wrinkle. He could hear nondescript noises coming from the kitchen. The cat started to enter the living room but must have changed its mind because of the smell and bolted into the library. It mewed, hissed, and then scampered into a closet settling on a bed made of linens. "Take your foot out." The dragon placed a sheet on the floor and a small towel. He dried the foot, and with a pair of tweezers, began to prod. The boy flinched. "Good, now I know where it is." But when the skin wouldn't release the glass, he went back into the kitchen, returning with a poultice of honey and baking soda. He applied the paste and wrapped the foot with a bandage. It was as secure as a cast. "We need to let it dry," he said. The boy looked at his foot and then back at the man. It was miraculous how he was able to work so efficiently, not a speck of powder or water had accidentally dropped or dripped.

"Can I go in there to wait?" the boy asked, pointing to the library.

The dragon looked to the room. "There aren't any chairs."

"I don't mind. I can sit on the floor and read."

A subtle nod offered permission. "She asleep?" he asked.

"No, at the beach."

"We don't want to disturb her then." He turned to the library. "Go on in if you want."

His attention to the room was at first drawn directly to the three glass tanks; however, unlike his sister, who had given him a detailed description, he was disappointed. A muslin cloth had been draped over each one with the intention of giving whatever was beneath a bit of privacy. He dragged his foot along the floor and putting his weight on the unbandaged foot, leaned into the bookshelf. They were from floor to ceiling tall, a colorful display of bindings, some in English and some in languages he was unfamiliar with. But unlike the public library, they were randomly shelved; however, what they appeared to have in common were their well-worn appearances. None were covered in a shiny jacket, but rather most a bit frayed on the edges as if having been pulled from the shelves many times. He was tired and now a bit annoyed that he wasn't lying on a cushion in the mountains. He shuffled his feet and moved sideways.

The Bell Jar. It was perched between *Flora and Fauna from the Court of Emperor Rudolf II* and *The Count of Monte Cristo* by Alexandre Dumas. It was a tight squeeze, but he managed to pull it free. *The Bell Jar*, a novel by Silvia Plath. He had a sudden change of heart toward the dragon. He opened the book and randomly leafed through the pages, but as if coming home to find a burglar in your home, he was confronted with a note that had been slipped between the pages. His hands trembled as he opened the paper, a piece of loose leaf with ragged edges that had been ripped free from a notebook. It was written in the same familiar handwriting. *Yoshi, what are you doing at the dragon's house? Be careful. Meet us tomorrow, same place, there are others. Adios amigo, Frito. Put this in your pocket and flush it!* He mocked the words "flush it" in his head.

"Time's up." It was the husky voice of the dragon. Guilt swept over the boy as he shoved Silvia Plath back on the shelf. He didn't remember, but he must have put the note in his pocket. The dragon was sitting on the living room floor with a clean towel. Saachi was still at the beach. His foot was stiff and now itchy. He sat across from the dragon with his leg out. Pieces of plaster-like poultice peeled off the bandage as it was unraveled. The dragon raised the foot by the heel and examined it. The boy heard the tweezers scrape across the shard, and with a quick prick, the sliver was pulled out. The dragon held it up between the tweezer.

"Let me see." The girl had gotten up and had put her face between the boy and the dragon. "See," she said. "I told you he could do it."

Get out of there now. "I guess we should get going. Thanks, thanks a lot." The boy rubbed his foot. It didn't hurt. He pulled his socks and shoes out from under the table and started to put them on.

"Did you see the fish?" she asked.

"No, it was resting."

"What about the frogs."

"They were resting too."

"I didn't know fish rested."

The dragon had gone into the kitchen and came back with two pieces of licorice. "Everything needs to rest."

"Can I come back and see them when they're awake." Her hand was on the knob, and her eyes were on the man.

The dragon nodded. He closed the door behind them and then reopened it. The black and white cat scurried outside and ran in the opposite direction.

"Do you like that cat," the girl asked.

"I suppose. Do you?"

"I suppose."

"Do you think Harriette is awake?"

He looked up at the sky. It was beginning to get a tinge of grey. "I suppose not. Want Chinese?"

The dragon was watching the boy and girl as they rounded the lawn home. He walked into the library and scanned the shelves. There was only one book out of place. With a poke of his finger, he aligned it, so it sat square with the others. "Time to wake up," he exclaimed. He slowly removed the cloth over each tank and then folded them into three neat bundles. He peered into the fish tank and smiled. "I don't blame you for being shy," he said. The fish swam to the top when they heard his voice. "I'm fixing dinner right now. You're having fresh oysters and bloodworms." A slapping of surface water breached the open tank, and he laughed. "You are playful when you're hungry, aren't you?"

CHAPTER 7

HIS MEMORY WAS sometimes fuzzy, but the chant remained distinctly intact. His father was summoned to the bedside of a young woman with brain fever. He was called together with others to pick up leaves from the tree. They were placed in the black pot of water and boiled. Pieces of yellow soap were scrapped from a bar with a pocketknife, and as the leaves bubbled, a sudsy stew was frothing into a thick poultice. He had turned away from the face as gashes were made on the woman's forehead. While the mixture cooled, the chant was repeated over and over, and when the poultice was spread over the forehead with his father's fingers, the chant took on a hushed fervor. A turban was wound around the woman's head, and the family took turns watching and chanting; endless chanting. He held a palm frond and waved it over the feverish woman. Finally, three days later, the fever broke. *AGO-É, AGO-YÉ, AGO-É. AGO-YÉ.* There was something Alice in Wonderland about his earliest memories: rabbits, queens, dark tunnels, and formalities with an undercurrent of magic. *This is for you. The sick woman removed her necklace and handed it to him. He wasn't going to take it, but she insisted, so he did.* The dragon had taken what didn't belong to him. He was too young to understand what it meant, so he hid the gift until he was old enough to understand. There had been a man who had died from wearing such a stolen object, but his was not a curse from theft. His was a fatal lure of a female.

"This is what happens when you spend your life in a memory," he reminded the cat. "How shall I entertain you?" But the cat remained asleep, which the dragon took as contentment.

* * *

THE LIBRARY FIXTURES created a goodly amount of light to read by. Frito took his seat at the head of the table. "One day we came home from school and found our mother drunk. My sister went outside to play. I went upstairs and took the pistol from my father's top drawer. A few minutes later I went outside and told Winnie, 'It was for the best.'" He looked around the table. Hawk nodded with the approval of someone who had heard the story many times. "When the doctor arrived, he said she was dead."

"Your mother?"

"She was always drunk," Gustave added.

"And Winnie? What did she say?"

"She said it was too bad she killed herself."

Yoshi whistled. "And your Dad?"

"What about him?"

What about him? Yoshi shrugged. It didn't seem like a strange question.

"This isn't about him."

"I guess not."

"Sometimes we have to protect the weaker and rescue them."

Yoshi assumed Frito saw himself as Winnie's hero. He thought about the girl, but she didn't seem weak, not in the way Winnie must be.

A doe-eyed boy had entered the room and leaned against the bookshelf behind the cubby of tables. He was examining the ragged group of boys with a hardened look. "He's one of us," said Gustave looking over his shoulder. A bruise looking like rotting fruit stained his right hand and ran up beneath his buttoned sleeves. "His name is Ivan."

Ivan stepped over to the table and sat down in an empty chair next to Hawk. "I'm Ivan," he said. It seemed like a funny thing to say since everyone already knew that.

"Today he will officially become one of us," explained Frito and then turned to Yoshi. "We want you to do the honors first." Ivan looked around the table and then set his eyes squarely on Yoshi.

"Honors?"

Hawk smiled. "You know."

Did he? What was he supposed to know? *Don't be stupid, you know...*
He couldn't look uncertain; he'd follow along and see what he was supposed
to do. "Oh, that." He elongated the words and smiled.

"Hawk, you and Gustave go with them."

They entered the men's room with a shared feeling of closeness that
relied on a few minutes of suffering, an affinity that is only possible between
siblings. "You don't wear a belt?" asked Hawk. Yoshi now knew what they
were talking about. He looked at Ivan. He hadn't noticed the boy had a
comic book sticking out of his pocket.

Yoshi nodded his head. "How about a shoe?"

"A shoe? That could work."

Summer of bruises. He removed his shoes and gave one of them to
Hawk. "You go after me, then Gustave, and I guess me again since Kojo
isn't here."

Ivan stood facing the stall. X-Man was facing them. "Isn't this where
I ask for a cigarette?"

They laughed.

"After I count to three, ready?"

"I'm already dead," he said.

And when it was over, Ivan exited the men's room like a game rooster
ready to do battle. The others followed behind, leaving Yoshi to put his shoe
back on.

* * *

NOW THERE WERE 5 brothers. Frito, Kojo, Gustave, Hawk, and Ivan.
Why weren't there any girls? "There are, it's just that we can't have girls in
the bathroom," explained the boy. The girl had to be told.

"Did you tell them about me?"

"They knew."

"Now what?"

He didn't have an answer. "I'm working on it."

"A guy came looking for you today."

"A guy?"

"A man."

"What man?"

"S something."

"Sikes?"

"Maybe."

"And Henrietta? Were her dactie krugers here?"

"Nocoo," she grinned.

"Is she in her room?"

"So many questions!" the girl moaned. "Yoyu, but she's not alone; the red-headed lady is in there."

The boy was quiet. He was tired. The morning had worn him out. He looked down at his shoes and retied the laces. Sikes had come to his house. He went behind the window curtain and looked out. The clouds were melting. A siren arrived before the ambulance stopped. A stretcher entered the neighbor's house and in a matter of minutes, came out. One of the men's shoulders shook as he carried the load to the back of the open door. The man inside closed the door, and they left."

"It's my fault," the girl said.

"How is it your fault."

"I buried the lemon water and salt in her yard. I should've taken them farther away."

He was sitting on the floor beside her and patted her knee. "She was kind of weird. It's not your fault. She walked around naked and stuff."

"I suppose so." The girl's voice had taken a dreary dip. The boy hoped she wasn't softening; her feeling guilty was not necessary. "Henrietta didn't even get up to see. How could she not have heard the ambulance?"

"Should we check on her?" he asked.

"You mean, look in her room?"

"Why not?" he stood up and beckoned for her to follow. But suddenly decided perhaps it wasn't such a good plan. The girl needed to be protected. "I was only kidding; she never hears anything when she has roogs."

"I'm going to the beach." She stood up and lifted the curtain. It fell back over her brother as she started for her room. "When you want supper, let me know." The door closed behind her.

The curtains were sheer enough for him to see through. A woman was standing in the living room with her hands on her hips, head back, and appeared to be talking, but he couldn't hear anything coming out of her mouth. It wasn't Henrietta or the redhead. She staggered over to the coffee table, picked through the ashtray, and found a cigarette butt with enough of a butt to light. It took several strikes and an equal amount of swearing to get the match lit. She was making a ceremony out of smoking, sucking hard, and then releasing the smoke with exaggerated, "ahhhhh's." She reminded the boy of a dog, the way she shook her head, like an old hound dog with a stick. Only the woman had a longer face.

"Bring the matches in here!" It was Henrietta.

He now got a better look at the woman as she rounded the table. She could have passed for a mannequin, but her behind was too big. "Soda?"

"No, just bring the damn matches!"

A putrid smell had emanated from the bedroom and filtered into the rest of the house. He was familiar with the scent, but it was stronger than usual. It was the smell of indifference. The mannequin leaned over the coffee table and swayed, scooping up the matches and then swaggering back to the bedroom. The door remained open for a few minutes and then slammed shut.

* * *

"I WOULD HAVE a dog, but there's a tax on them." The boy looked perplexed. "You can't just have a dog, you got to own it. And if you own it, then you need to get a license."

"Like a car?"

"Like a car." He leaned his face into the sun. "Sure is hot."

The boy observed Sikes more closely. Beneath his leathery skin was a well-chiseled jaw and fair eyes. Today he was sockless. "I can get you some clothes if you want."

"What kind of clothes?"

"Just some stuff we have that nobody needs anymore."

"Any shoes? Cause I could really use a new pair of shoes. Size 11 would be best, but I can wear a half size smaller if they're leather. Leather stretches."

"If you want, I can get them for you today."

He sat up and turned to the boy. "How'd you know I was here?"

"It's Tuesday. There's the book club on Tuesdays, and I figured you'd be here."

He laughed. "Free coffee and doughnuts?"

"Something like that. I like the chocolate ones."

"I can see," he pointed to the boy's stained shirt. "Chocolate is good." The man picked up his backpack and stretched. "I was at your house the other day. Met your sister, unless that was your girlfriend."

Yoshi made a sour face. "Girlfriend! No, she's just my sister. She told me."

"I was hungry, so I figured I'd take you up on your generous offer."

"I can get you something to eat too, if you're hungry."

"What've you got?"

"Leftover Chinese."

"Not rice, leftover rice is lousy."

"I agree." He lied. "Egg roll. You can have my egg roll."

Sikes pulled a small flattened spiral pad from his back pocket and turned a few pages. "Seems that I have no other engagements," and flipping it closed shoved it back.

They left the meditation garden just as a scowling codger was entering. *"Murder's kid."* The boy glanced up at the man walking beside him, hoping he hadn't heard the remark. It appeared he hadn't. Sikes briskly walked the whole way home with his hands in his pockets and his backpack strapped across his shoulder.

There was a weed path leading to the basement window where from the inside, you had a view of passing feet belonging to bodies cut off from sight. Once inside, the darkness of the sealed hole extended beneath the floor above into a large gloomy room. The boy squatted down and pointed to the mud-stained window. "I'll go in and open it up, you wait here." The man examined the window.

"Kind of a tight fit, don't you think?"

"Not if you shimmy in backward, feet first. My mother's sick and can't be disturbed." The man nodded. He sat on the ground with his head resting against the clapboard. He wondered if this cloak and dagger game was worth an egg roll. His sneakers were worn at the tips of the soles, and his stomach was wrapped in a toga of hunger. He would wait.

When he went in, he could tell something had once gone wrong. Enamel pots like white skulls sat on the landing of the stairwell. An old mattress and headboard leaned against the wall. A half-dozen paint cans and roller pans were sitting on drop cloths. He followed the boy, where the air smelled dirty. The furnace and washing machine, fuse-box, and heater occupied the same space. "You can look through this," he said, standing before a sizable cardboard box. *I haven't seen you in a long time, are you giving him the clothes?* Yoshi nodded yes and then peeled back the flaps.

Sikes pulled from off the top a turtleneck sweater, ski hat, and tweed jacket. He set them aside. "We were going to give them away." The boy lied.

"These will come in handy for winter." He kneeled down and rooted headlong among the clothes until he pulled out a pair of work boots. He turned them over and then felt the inside.

"He didn't wear sneakers," the boy said.

"What's this?" handing him a small tight bundle.

"Socks. It's the best way to keep the pairs together." Yoshi unraveled and wriggled them before the man. Sikes grinned and took to scavenging the bottom of the box before tossing six sock-balls into his backpack with the boots. "This will do for now," he said.

Yoshi wanted to say something meaningful. "It's a pretty good cellar. I think we had rats only once."

"What happened to them?'

"A guy came and set traps."

"Traps, that'll do it."

"I'm going up to get the egg roll," but Sikes didn't answer. He was unfolding an aluminum lawn chair. He shook it before sitting down, pushing on the fraying straps.

"I'll be here." He sat down and rested his feet on the cardboard box. "Got a good view." He pointed to the window.

You're leaving him alone? "I've got a headache, leave me alone," the boy thought as he climbed the stairs. The voice in his head stopped as he nudged the door open, but it reopened after a few minutes. "Come on up."

Sikes started up slowly, contemplating whether he should follow the boy. He stopped short of walking into the hallway; his large head leaning to one side and the weight of the backpack exaggerated his posture with a tilt to the left. He trailed the boy into the kitchen.

"Why the change of plans?"

"No one's home. My mother is at the doctor's." He lied. "I think there's a poncho in the hall closet that would fit you. I could put it in a bag if you want."

"That would be very accommodating of you, Yoshi. One can never tell when it might rain. What color is it?"

"Yellow."

"Yellow is good, grey would be better, but yellow is good too." His eyes were on the refrigerator as he spoke.

"You can sit here, it's where I usually sit." The man reached for the chair and pulled it away from the table. There was a partially eaten bowl of cereal. He lifted it to his mouth and slurped it down. He set the bowl aside. "I just assumed no one was going to finish this?"

"No, she was done." Imagining Henrietta entering the room, Yoshi pointed to the kitchen clock. "My mom will be home soon. Maybe I should put the egg roll in the bag with the poncho."

Sikes looked gratefully at the boy, "It's strange for me too," he said. He got up and pushed the chair in while Yoshi pulled from under the sink a grocery bag. The visitor's eyes hunted around the room, following the boy to the broom closet. The poncho was hanging on a peg. "It'll fit," he said and opened the bag. He deposited the poncho along with the egg roll. "Here."

Sikes slung his backpack over his shoulder and took the paper bag crumpling it closed. "Mind if I use the can before I go?"

"Can?"

"The bathroom."

"Right, the can. It's over there. The one after the cellar door." Yoshi waited a few minutes outside the door before deciding it was awkward when he heard the toilet flush. "I'll meet you in the basement."

"Okay."

He could hear the water in the basin filling as he walked downstairs. He wrote his name in the dust and crossed it out. His old basketball was in the corner. He rolled it out and tried to see if it would bounce. It wouldn't. His sister's dollhouse was now a collection of rusting metal, and the miniature residents' faces and clothes had faded with time. The cellar door shut with the voice of Sikes entering. "I would have shaved, but I couldn't find a razor." His hair was slicked back, having been dunked in water.

"You can come back again if you want."

The street-sleeper tossed the paper bag and his backpack through the window first. "I don't suppose you have a ladder." But it didn't take him long to hoist himself up and out the narrow space. "He dipped down and stuck his head through the opening. "Be sure to close this," he said. "We don't want rats."

Yoshi stood with his face raised to the window. *Did you flush the note?* He put his hand in his pocket and turned it inside out. There was

nothing but lint. He looked around the room and rolled the basketball top-
pling the beach chair over.

CHAPTER 8

"WHAT THE HELL is this?" Rory shook the bag at the woman. "I'm tired, Rory, leave me alone." She rolled over, but he didn't give her time to pull the covers up because he turned the sack over and dumped the contents out onto her stomach. "What the hell are you doing?"

"What are you trying to pull?"

"Shit, what is this?" she yanked the bedding to the floor and straightened up.

"That's what I want to know!"

"Where'd you get this?"

"From you!"

"Me?"

"Yes, don't you remember? You left this for me." He rattled the empty bag and then lifted the rain poncho for her to see. "Where's my shit?" His breathing was rapid while trying to control his anger.

Henrietta stared at the poncho. "I don't know." She pulled her fingers through her hair and tried to remember. She rolled to the side of the bed and reached for the cigarette pack. It was empty. She crushed it in her hands and tossed it down with disgust. Then she turned with contempt. "It seems that you picked up the wrong bag, asshole."

"What the hell was a poncho doing in a bag, unless someone is friggin' with you?"

But hard as she tried, no recollection of the past few days would reconcile the exchange. "Shit!" The dullness of her thoughts translated into her own carelessness. "Give me a minute," she said, "and get the hell out of my room."

"A minute," he repeated.

"Wait, you got a cigarette?"

He tossed a pack on her bed and walked out. Her bony fingers reached in and pulled a cigarette free. Her hand was shaking as she tried to light the match. She strained with both hands and tilted the tip until it touched the flame. She caught a glimpse of herself in the mirror. A colorless form collided with her reflection. She leaned in and blew smoke up into her nostrils. "I love that trick." She smiled and then frowned. "This is such a waste," she told herself. She was going to have to offer Rory her cut. Such a damn waste. She took another drag and put the cigarette out. Then she lay back down. She pulled the sheet up and closed her eyes when she heard someone come in. She didn't have to open them to know who it was.

"What the hell are you doing? A minute is up."

"Go away."

"Not until we get this fixed."

"I'll make it up to you, Rory. Now leave me the hell alone."

She could feel him leaning over her, his face nearly touching hers. She could feel him breathing. His breath reeking of tobacco and peanuts, his neck smelling from cheap cologne. Then, in a split second, he screamed. "Shit, you bit me! You bitch, you bit my nose."

Her eyes remained closed, unable to see the stunned victim as he protected his face with his hands. "Are you bleeding?"

He opened his palms. "No, but it hurts! You bit my damn nose."

"That my dear boy was not a bite; more of a nip. Consider yourself lucky. Now get the hell out of my room and let me sleep." The woman remained motionless while Rory was feeling sorry for himself and shut the door behind him.

"What happened to your nose?"

"Your mother bit it," he said.

"What did you do?"

"Nothing." He was holding the poncho in his hand.

The boy tried not to act surprised. "Where'd you get that?"

"It got in a bag by mistake. Is it yours?"

He shook his head no. "What are you going to do with it?"

"Throw it away, it's just a dirty poncho."

"It doesn't look dirty to me."

"Here, I don't want it. You can have it."

"Is she up?"

Rory turned to the bedroom and shook his head. "Vampires don't get up till midnight." He winked.

* * *

"MAYBE SHE REALLY is a vampire," said the girl.

"Don't be dexif, vampires don't bite noses."

"Maybe her aim was off."

"If she's a vampire, then how come we're not?" He hoped his logic was correct.

"She actually bit his nose? What did it look like?"

"Red. Very red and raw. Red and raw."

The girl made a face. "Must have been some badass roogs." She paused. "There must be something we can do."

"Do?"

"Just in case," she looked at him. Now he was being dense. "In case she's a..."

"Bat!" he laughed.

"It isn't funny; no, a vampire. Now you're the dexif." She smiled. She liked getting even.

* * *

"ONLY A SMALL amount of powder is needed," the dragon said as he sprinkled a pinch into a clay bowl. "If all the power remains on the surface instead of mixing with the water, then she is what you believe. If the power does not mix, then she is as she remains."

"What was that stuff?"

"He called it Great Bird medicine."

"Like a turkey?"

"I don't know," the girl said.

"And what happened?"

"It floated."

The boy shrugged. "Then, I guess she just wanted to bite him."

"I guess so."

* * *

WHEN HENRIETTA WOKE up, she was bleary-eyed. It took a minute for her to remember the incident a few hours earlier. Yellow was the first color that came to mind. She leaned over the night table and reached for a cigarette, but her mouth was too dry to get any enjoyment from smoking before drinking some water. She stared up at the ceiling, and then she laughed. *I did bite the bastard. Served him right for getting too close.* There was a faint whisper in her head, a question that needed an answer. "Who's been in the house?" She needed to take inventory. As for stealing, of course, they will take things that don't belong to them if they're sure of not being caught, but this is not the main cause of their degradation. Stealthily and cat-like, they tap on the wooden door, which, as if by its own free will, swings open and closes hiding them from view. Who had trouble raising money? *I know the boy to be a liar, but he does behave.* Clouds of doubt washed over her. *He was the only other person to have access to the garden. On the other hand, maybe she was being too hasty. If he wanted to mutiny, he and the girl would have done it already. He had too much of her in his blood to have deceived her.* "I need a cigarette," she screamed. "I know one of you is home! Bring me a glass of water too!"

The moment the boy entered, it was obvious that she was grossly annoyed. "Where's the bag meant for Rory?" Her eyes were her most telling feature, and also the wickedest; and when she looked at him, he felt that she was piercing his character. He set the cup of water on the nightstand.

"Your cigarettes are here." He picked up the pack from the floor and handed it to her.

"Go bla, bla. Blaa, blaa?" She was shouting.

The boy struck the match and cupped his hand while she lit her cigarette.

"Bla, bla, bla Rory?" She sucked hard on the filter.

She was different when she was angry. Her head seemed larger than it was yesterday. He knew his reply would be either Yes or No. "If I say no, then I will present the truth as a pleasing untruth. Then maybe her head will return to normal," he thought. "No," he said.

"And the poncho?"

"I think in the broom closet."

Her face relaxed. It had become apparent that her attitude against the poncho was not his doing. She now owned a private association with the word, and the boy had been absolved of the crime.

"Well, somehow Rory got the wrong bag."

The boy was faced with a decision to leave the room or stay. If he stayed, he could help Henrietta carry on. If he left the room, she would carry on. He shrugged his shoulders. "I don't know why Rory made a mistake." A hungry pause settled between them. Her head had finally been reduced to its usual size. He started to walk out when he noticed a strange odor. "Do you smell something funny?"

She sniffed. "Maybe it's your socks. Did you change your socks?"

He looked down at his feet. "I'm not wearing socks."

"Then it's not your socks. Be sure to change your socks. You can get stink foot if you don't."

"No, it doesn't smell like feet," he thought. But it wasn't until he was standing in the hallway that he recognized the stench; it was indifference.

CHAPTER 9

I T WAS A rainy afternoon when the boy, zipping up the yellow poncho and obscuring his head beneath the hood, began his walk to the library. The mud lay thick along the sidewalk cracks, and everyone he passed stepped between the puddles. A thin man wearing a green raincoat looked like a reptile as he emerged from his house. *"Dog killer."*

The boy exchanged words, "No she's not!" But the slimy man was too hard of hearing to take notice. The boy followed the mud-stained sidewalk, and when the rain finally stopped, he pulled the hood off his head and entered the open glass doors. The librarian was busy placing reserved books onto the cart and didn't see him file past to the shelf, leaving the only clue of his arrival, wet footprints. He peeled the poncho off and rolled it up under a chair. It was an uncomfortable skin of clothes to wear. On his walk to the library, he kept thinking of *The Bell Jar,* and now, as he reached up, his hand fell short of finding the book. It was missing. He was clinging to an orderly arrangement of books, but the system failed like a buoy that has drifted.

"Excuse me."

The librarian's eyes lifted.

"Can you tell me where *The Bell Jar* is."

"It's not on the shelf?"

"No."

"Then, it must be checked out."

"Checked out?"

"Yes. Do you want me to put a reserve on it for you?"

"Reserve?"

"We can call you when it comes back in."

"No, that's okay."

"It's no problem, I just need your library card."

He didn't have a card. "It's okay."

"I can see when it is due back."

But he didn't wait around for her to check. Instead, he went to the men's room where a note was taped to the mirror behind the door. It was folded with his name printed on the outside, Yoshi. *Dear amigo, I guess you figured out that Silvia Plath is missing. She should be back in a few weeks. We can meet tomorrow at noon behind the library by the benches. Be careful of that guy you were with. Frito. P.S. Flush after reading.* He crumpled the note into a ball and tossed it into the toilet. He didn't think he had to be told to flush. The lights flickered, and then without waiting, he pulled the lever and watched the paper get sucked down the drain.

The poncho was under the chair where he had left it. "Hey, kid." He turned to see who it was. "Why don't you have a library card?" No one was there. He had a headache. He unraveled the poncho and pulled it down over his head. His footprints had all dried up, but his sneakers still felt wet. He wondered if Sikes missed having the poncho. He'd give it back to him when they met again.

* * *

SOMEWHERE BETWEEN THE knowledge of ideas and the all-knowing, there is a space in-between. Maybe it's the territory of angels or spirits or friends nobody else can see. These invisible entities know things that ordinary humans cannot. The boy had room in his head, and so he let them in.

* * *

HENRIETTA OCCUPIED A large amount of space, not physical space; it was her presence that was extensive. "She's everywhere," the boy said. "Kind of like a storm cloud blotting out all the light."

Hawk laughed.

"It's true," the boy said.

"So, what are you going to do about it?" Kojo kicked a small stone.

"I haven't decided exactly."

"You need to make a plan. We all have." Frito pulled his sunglasses up on to his forehead and winked.

"I'm working on it."

"Not with that guy. You gotta be careful who you trust." Kojo had collected small stones and was pitching them at the base of the statue.

"You can't make shit up as you go. That's what they do."

"They?"

"Parents, they react. You need to be calculated. The first thing for survival is money. Number two is you gotta stash some away. And number three is you need a steady income to exist. That's why your situation is different."

Yoshi leaned forward and rested his elbows on his knees. He turned his head. "How so?"

"We all have another adult under control. But you don't. The only adult in your house is Henrietta."

"Which means?"

"Which means where will you get money?" Frito's statement sounded obviously pessimistic. "We can help, but you'll need a solid plan." Frito moved over to let Hawk sit down. "After money, you'll want a permeant solution to your problem."

"Sometimes, if you're lucky, things take their natural course," Hawk explained. "Like an arrest or overdose."

"But you, Yoshi, you have to be very, very careful. If anyone finds out Henrietta is gone, they'll take you and your sister away. That's why whatever plan you come up with, it must be a secret. It must be a secret forever."

The boy felt sick to his stomach. Things were happening too fast, and his head was aching.

"You look pretty bad," Kojo said.

"I feel like shit."

"Honesty can do that. We just wanted to let you know from our experiences."

They had been sitting in the garden for what seemed all day. "Tell him about the rules of The Colony," said Kojo.

"Colony?"

"Yeah, that's what we are, a colony. Not a colony like the 13 colonies. We're like a bacteria colony. To be more exact, a colony in biology is where two or more individuals are in close association with one another for the mutual benefit, such as stronger defense or the ability to attack bigger prey."

The boy was impressed with Hawk's definition.

"You already know rule number 1," said Frito. *Memorize the note and then flush it.* Rule 2: *Don't trust anyone not like us.* Rule 3: *Everything said and done is kept a secret.* Rule 4: *No one is above another in The Colony.* Rule 5: *Squealers are subject to pain.*"

The words hit him like a concussion.

"If we're finished, then we should go," said Kojo. He had made a small collection of small stones at the base of the statue.

Frito stood up. "Until the book is returned, I'll put the note under those stones. By then, you will have a solution." He put his hand on Yoshi's shoulder. "See you later, amigo."

They all left, and the boy was alone. He was supposed to be feeling good. Sikes was the only person he really liked in such a long time. *Rule 2: Don't trust anyone not like us.* It was just that he felt different about Sikes. *Shut up, shut up, shut up!* He put his hands over his ears and waited until he happened upon a butterfly landing on a flower. He took his hands away from his ears and listened. He was sure he could hear the fluttering of the wings as it hovered over the plant. It was a gentle humming. His head didn't hurt anymore. "Thank you," the boy whispered.

"*You're welcome.*"

* * *

SIKES RETURNED TO the house. The black and white cat was lurking around when he squatted by the basement window and peered in. He pulled a dried strip of rubber. It easily broke free from the corner of the window where he pulled gently. He slipped his fingers in and dropped an envelope. He thought he saw it land near the washing machine, but he couldn't be sure, it was too dark. Then he got up and passed back through the yard. Whatever secrets were going on in the house, he could only guess. A few drops of rain began to fall as he walked. His only regret was he hadn't kept the poncho.

When the girl, carrying the basket of clothes, stepped up to the washing machine, she saw the envelope addressed to Yoshi. She wanted to open it, but it was sealed. She folded it and put it in her back pocket and stuffed it down so it wouldn't be sticking out. She didn't mind doing laundry, it was the sorting that she hated. She liked her mother's sheets, they had small flowers, pink and yellow with matching pillowcases. She had decided a long time ago that she would have flowered sheets when she got older. But her mother hadn't given her the sheets to wash, this load was towels. The grey one smelled like a wet dog. She turned on the machine and watched as the soap suds began to crawl up the barrel. Next time she would add less detergent.

Yoshi was unzipping the poncho when she got upstairs. "I found this next to the washing machine." She handed him the envelope.

"Is she home?"

"No."

"Where'd she go?"

The girl shrugged. "Just said she had to go out." She pointed to the envelope. "Open it."

"Did she say when she was coming back."

"No."

He pulled a knife from the drainboard and slit the envelope. "It's money!" He opened the envelope wider and counted out five twenty-dollar bills along with a note, written around a newspaper car ad like a frame. *Thanks, here's your share. Sikes.*

"A hundred dollars!"

The boy looked and then smiled. "Want pizza, extra cheese, and a large bottle of soda!"

The very existence of the money provoked the question. "Who's Sikes?"

"Extra cheese?"

"Yes, and pepperoni. Is he the guy looking for you?"

"Yeah, the one I met at the library. I wanted to give him some of the old clothes in the basement. He only wanted shoes. I remembered the yellow poncho, so I put it in a paper bag for him but must have taken the bag with the tobler's roogs."

"Is Sikes a gryphon?"

"I don't think so. Maybe a roreg, like Henrietta. That's how come I got the money. He split the sale with me. But he doesn't get yarmied."

"How do you know?"

"I just do."

She pursued her own thoughts behind his blind acceptance and moved on. "I'm going to make a fresh lemon mixture after I bury the old one."

"Next door?"

"Well, it can't do any more harm. When she comes back from the hospital, I'll find another place to bury it."

"Do you think it works?"

"Henrietta didn't bite us, did she."

The girl went into her bedroom with the knife and salt. In a few minutes, she came out and set the bowl on the kitchen table before heading to Yoshi's room."

"Where are you going."

"To get your bowl."

"I didn't know I had one."

"You don't look under your bed."

Under the bed? She put shit under the bed. He put his hand on the back of his neck and squeezed it hard. *Shut up, she's my sister! Shut up! It's my house, and I make the rules. Rule number 1: Kinship is to protect. Rule 2: Doing evil is not always evil.* "I have a warped conscience," he said when she returned to the kitchen.

"Want to come with me?" She waited for him to open the door. "Bring the little trowel and meet me around back," she said as she slipped outside.

She didn't use the exact same burial site, but rather, scratched away the dirt and began to dig a new hole. The ground was soft and relatively easy to unearth.

"Do we say something before you cover it up?" he asked.

She poured the mixture into the hole and watched as the soil sucked up the water and salt. "I'm not sure; I never said anything before. Do you think we should?"

"It might make it work better if we do."

She hadn't thought about it. "We should ask the dragon." She twisted her head in the direction of his house.

"You go. I'll put the stuff away."

She patted the earth with her hands and clapped the dirt free. "Okay." The boy stood watching as his sister wondered towards the man's porch. The dragon had a comfortable porch, it faced east. If the sun were an ocean, it would spray yellow froth on the steps each morning as the light rolled up and back under the shade of the roof like the tide. There was no particular pattern to the filled-in holes the girl had made. He stepped over them on his way back to the house and wondered how big a hole it would take to bury a person.

* * *

"WHERE'S YOUR SISTER?" Henrietta was sitting at the kitchen table, picking at the leftover toast from his breakfast.

"Outside."

"Where outside?"

"I guess to play."

"Then you'll have to go," there was disgust in her voice that she didn't try to disguise. "I need you to take this check and cash it at the bank."

"There's money in the jar if you need it."

"I need more."

"To pay Rory?" Suddenly he felt emboldened. Her head looked smaller than usual.

"If you must know, yes. So here," she handed him the check. "Be sure to bla bla bla bla!"

"Okay," he took it and folded it before securing into his pocket.

"Don't forget; bla bla bla!"

"I won't," he agreed and smiled before shutting the door. *Funny how her eyes suddenly popped out when she got mad.*

Before getting on the teller's line, he stood in the lobby before a wooden desk and picked up the pen. It was attached to a small chain. He pulled a withdrawal slip from the bin and started to write; the pen didn't work. He moved over to a different pen. This time it worked. He looked at the signature on the check and tried his hand at copying. The only letter that gave him any difficulty was the scrawled H. He practiced a few more times before crumpling up the paper and tossing it into the bin. Maybe the girl would be better at it, she had good handwriting.

When he arrived home, Henrietta wasn't answering his knocks on the door, so he put the money in the jar. He was supposed to water the garden. Light was bleeding out from under the door, and he wondered if he had forgotten to snap the lock the last time because it was unhinged. If anyone were careless, it would have been Henrietta. He pushed lightly against the door. "Hello, amigo." It was Frito.

"How'd you get in?"

"I can pick any lock," explained Ivan. "Well, most locks, but your house was open, so it was pretty easy. We just opened the door."

"You don't mind, do you?" Frito asked almost apologetically.

"We thought you might need help with your problem. Mine's taken care of." There was something sinister in the way Ivan spoke that made Yoshi uncomfortable.

"So soon?"

Frito clasped his hands together and stretched. "Yep, an anonymous call to social services; it took a few times, but they finally got to his house.

"I'm feeling free already. Court date is in a few months."

The boy didn't remember the bruised cheek when they were introduced. "What happened?" he asked, pointing to Ivan's face.

"The other day, I put some soap in the whiskey, and my drunk father ended up leaning over the toilet for more than an hour with his finger down his throat. When he was finished puking, he came out and wanted a little more whiskey to take away the bad taste out of his mouth. I poured him a shot glass full, but this time with a teaspoonful of baking powder in it. His throat got so raw that he couldn't talk. Then he knocked my ass to the floor."

"Oh," said Yoshi. "Looks like it hurts."

"Why is this one empty?" Frito poked his finger into the soil.

"It was harvested. But there are seeds planted that I need to water." The two visitors watched as Yoshi prepared the bottles and began to spray the earth. "Those over there are still too small to get picked."

"You do realize you're an enabler."

"Enabler?" He stopped watering.

"Yea, by taking care of these plants. What you wanna do is inhibit. Unless of course," Frito smiled cunningly, "you have another idea."

"I'm working on it." He lied. "In fact, I'll have something to report the next time we meet."

Ivan was bored wandering between the planters. "They look like giant bathtubs filled with dirt."

"I can finish later." Yoshi put the water bottle aside as they followed him out of the room.

"What's down there?" The cellar door was ajar inviting Ivan to open it wider.

"Laundry stuff and the furnace."

"I hate cellars," Ivan said.

There was a strained moment at the back door as the two visitors descended the stops. Yoshi wanted them to stay but decided it would be better if they left. He closed the door and wondered what their houses were like. *There are others like us. Only some are more pathetic than others.*

CHAPTER 10

"**W**HY IS SHE out here?"

"I don't know, maybe we should look."

The boy trailed the girl to the mother's room, where the door was open wide enough to see inside. "Toblers," she said. "They're all yarmied."

The boy pushed her aside and looked in. Then he turned away. "It smells weird."

"I haven't decided what I want for breakfast," said the girl.

"What about her?" He pointed to Henrietta lying on the couch. Her mouth half-open, snoring every other breath. "What's she sleeping on?"

The girl tiptoed closer. "A tablecloth."

He nodded in agreement. "Want some cereal?" He handed her the box from off the coffee table.

She dug in and removed a handful. "It's almost empty." She plopped herself in the armchair and began to pick at the flakes one at a time from her palm. All the while, they both stared at the sleeping woman.

"Do you think her head looks big?"

The girl twisted her neck to the side. "Maybe, a little bigger. I think it's her hair."

"Not me, if you block out her hair, I see a bigger head. Her hair always looks like that."

Yoshi reached for the cereal and shook the box before pouring some into his hand. He set the box back. "I think she's waking up," he whispered.

"What time is it?" The mother stretched her legs.

"Around nine," said the boy.

"Day or night."

"Day," said the girl.

Henrietta's tranquility had been disturbed. Her eyes were glazed and watery, and she wore an idiotic expression. She moved slowly as if her limbs were powerless while she tried to sit up. She tugged at the tablecloth, but it was not long enough to fold over her shoulders. She started to stand, but the floor beneath her feet seemed to slip as she took a step. "What the hell are you two staring at?" But they didn't answer because it was obvious. "I'm going back to my room!" she complained and took a small step forward. But to walk with steadiness would take effort she didn't have and tottered from side to side while her legs appeared inadequate to sustain any balance. "Someone is coming by later to pick up a bag."

"Is it going to be Rory? the boy asked.

But she didn't answer him.

"Well, that went well," said the girl. She got up and dusted her hands on her shirt. "I'm going to get some water."

The boy followed and sat down at the kitchen table. He shoved aside the dirty plates and put his elbows on the table with his head in his hands. "We need to talk." He looked up. His sister was picking through the sink for the cleanest glass she could find. "We have an egmol, an onder egmol."

"About?" She ran the water and filled the glass.

"Henrietta. She's a gryphon and a roreg."

"And a tobler," Saachi added.

"Great," the boy said sarcastically. "Roreg, egmol, and tobler." He shook his head again as if the entire world was on his watch.

"So, how is it our egmol?" She drank the water and then put the glass back in the sink, balancing it between two bowls. "How is it our egmol?" she asked again.

"Look around."

She pulled the chair away and sat down. "I don't want to, so I won't." Her eyes were fixed on his face. She was determined not to blink.

"There are others like us," he remaindered her.

"Then that's good. I think I'm going to read a book. The dragon let me borrow one."

"What book?"

"Mythology. If you want me, I'll be behind the curtain." She stood up and patted him on his back.

* * *

YOSHI WOKE UP from a dream, and the first thing he said was, "Shit!" Then he got up from the couch and stood in front of the curtain.

"I'm reading," she said.

"How long was I asleep?"

"About ten minutes."

"Is that all."

"Yep."

"Do you think the dragon is home?"

"He's always home," she said.

"I'll be right back."

"I'll be here."

The dragon was on his porch when the boy walked up the steps. "Do you want some lemonade?"

It was warm outside. The boy nodded yes, and they went into the house. The cat followed with her pair of kittens.

"What happened to the screen door?"

"They tried to climb it," the dragon said, pointing to the tiny felines. "Troublemakers."

Yoshi was directed to the living room, where he sat on the floor and leaned against the plush cushions. In a few minutes, the man returned with a tall glass of iced lemonade and offered it to the boy. He was a large man, and Yoshi was impressed in the way he nimbly folded himself onto the floor.

"I had this really weird dream," he explained before taking a sip of the drink. It tasted tarter than he liked.

The dragon looked back blankly, waiting for him to begin, and then closed his eyes as if he were going to be told a bedtime story.

Taking the man's cue, he began to reveal his dream. "My sister and I were in a store where they sell fake arms and legs to people that have lost their limbs, like in an accident or in the war. We had to walk down several flights of stairs and enter a large room that was more like a basement. It was dim except for a few light bulbs hanging from the ceiling. The room was empty except for only one very long table displaying hands and feet and legs and arms and eyeballs in all sizes and colors. We kept walking around and around looking for just the right ones when all of a sudden, my sister says, 'what are we doing, she's not even dead.' And then I woke up."

The dragon waited a moment before opening his eyes. The boy was making an annoying noise by sucking on ice. "Is that it?"

"Yeah, kind of weird, isn't it?"

"I imagine it was a bit frightening," said the dragon. His voice did not offer any intonation. Instead, it was flat, considering the account he had just heard. "What do you want me to do about it?"

Yeah, what do you want him to do about it? "I just thought, maybe, well, you might know what it means," Yoshi said.

"Tell me," asked the dragon. "Are you unprincipled?"

The boy was confused. "I don't know what you mean."

"My opinion is only human, reason is absolute." He paused to reflect. "But there is a link between the two."

The boy was not sure where his dream fit into this mumbo-jumbo, and now he was sorry he even brought it up. "I'm afraid that I don't get it."

"Reason has no face, it's a state of mind. It often resides in the background. The reason for your dream may have nothing to do with any one thing except a glorious imagination. On the other hand, it could be an outburst of your inner secrets. At least the table in your dream wasn't a banquet hall." He appealed to the boy's sense of humor. Yoshi smiled. "Dreams cannot be rescued; many are absurd with a few fragments of images that deserve attention." The dragon was finished talking and pulled himself up from the floor. "Would you like more lemonade?"

The boy's stomach was feeling more like it had been coated in an acid bath. "No, no, thanks." His attention turned to the library since the dream interpretation was a bust.

"You may go in if you want. We have a few more fish you might like to see. The new ones are smaller but quite aggressive. They need to be better behaved."

We, who is he talking about? Yoshi laughed at the last remark. He handed the dragon back the glass and stood up. The door to the library was wide open, and he could see that cloth once covering the tanks had all been lifted.

"Go in if you want, I have some things to do in the kitchen. Your sister found a book. Maybe you will too." The dragon retrieved back to the kitchen while Yoshi entered the library. *He ran your dream through a sieve and left you with a few crumbs. At least he didn't spit on it.* The boy put his hands over his ears and then moved them up to his temples. His head was the same size. *Go on, you know he has a copy of what you're looking for. The Bell Jar* was on the shelf just as he remembered. The book fell from the shelf effortlessly this time. He kept his back to the open door and shuffled through the pages. There was no note. Only a bookmark had been shoved between the pages where a light pencil mark had underlined a sentence. "I thought the most beautiful thing in the world must be shadow." He put the marker back in and placed the book on the shelf. The day had been an accumulation of symbols, none of which made any sense. He wondered why the sentence was underlined. Maybe it was a random game, a finger running up the page, and then stopping. *Reason is absolute.* What now? He must go home. He walked carefully, stepping around the black tiles on the floor to the doorway. He didn't want to fall in.

"Leaving without a book?" asked the dragon.

"Maybe next time."

"Give these to your sister," he said, offering a muslin pouch secured with twine. "Seeds. They'll produce beautiful flowers. But just in case you want to, don't eat any."

"Poisonous?"

"Very."

"Does she need any lemons?"

"No, I don't think so." The dragon was wearing a silk shirt and a pair of billowy pants. He looked very comfortable. "Thanks," said the boy and shook the small pouch.

"A ragged artist can paint just as good a picture as one that is well-dressed."

"I'll remember," said the boy. He shut the screen door and bounded down the steps. He still didn't know what the hell the dragon was talking about.

* * *

HE ARRIVED HOME, and like the next turn of the kaleidoscope, Saachi was waiting in the kitchen, wearing a rose-colored ribbon in her hair. "The new guy showed up. His name's in here." She handed the black book to Yoshi. "Rory got crossed out. She wrote the new tobler's name above."

"Where'd you find this?"

"In the bathroom."

He glanced at the page and then snickered. "Arp?"

The girl smiled. "He didn't look like an Arp. Looked more like a Dick."

"What did he say?"

"Thanks."

"Is she up?"

"I don't think so. The other gryphons left when I was at the beach. What's that?" She reached for the muslin sack.

"It's for you from the dragon. Seeds."

Her eyes lit up. "He remembered! Now we can plant something ourselves," she explained.

"Outside?"

"No, dexif. In the garden." She tugged at the twine until the pouch opened and pinched a few seeds between her fingers. "You're in charge of watering. They won't take up much space." He wore a look of disapproval. "Oh, come-on. Don't be dactie."

"What if she finds out."

"She won't. She never goes in there anymore."

"I suppose it couldn't hurt. She wouldn't have any reason not to believe us."

So, in the solitude of the afternoon, they took a trip to the garden, to the room where their ideals ran unparallel to the mother's but magnetized by the same pole; self-satisfaction. When they finished, the boy watered the seeds that lay beneath the soil between the larger plants. "What do you suppose happened to Rory?" asked the girl. Yoshi snapped the padlock shut.

"Maybe, he's eept."

"Maybe. But how?"

Such an idea of "how" was to venture into dangerous territory. "Shot like the dog."

"Nocoo," the girl disagreed. "I bet he's just yarmied somewhere. He got more cabbu from Henrietta. He could buy a lot of roogs with all that cabbu."

The boy's dedication to solving their problem put him in a dilemma. The militant attitude of The Colony offered no leniency. And why should it? He valued their secrets; they were like him. Theirs was a world in opposition to the norm. They were supposed to perform normally; but, how could they? They were outliers in an anthology of childhood. For the boy, secrets were a natural form of concealment, but not necessarily deceptive. A tapping on the back door broke his thoughts. He turned to his sister, and she whispered, "Roreg?" He shrugged and waited. They had no reason to become alarmed, yet he felt acutely wary of the intrusion. "Answer it," she said. So he did.

"Give this to your mother." A small parcel was handed to the boy through the open door. The girl filed behind to see who it was standing in the threshold. The voice was low and impertinent.

"A donkey face," thought the girl, and she wanted to laugh but stepped back behind the boy when the man handed him a stern warning.

"You'll be sure she gets it." He gave a counterfeit smile and rubbed his hands together in a conciliatory manner.

Yoshi nodded, yes. He clutched the package feeling strangely anguished.

"Good," the stranger replied and offering no emotion turned away. His crafty eyes had roused the suspicions of both.

The girl moaned after the back door was shut. "Roogs," she said. "It has to be roogs."

The boy raised his eyes languidly and tossed the package on the kitchen table. "Do you think you could forge Henrietta's signature?"

"Like a witwit?" she asked with great enthusiasm.

"I guess they do forgery from time to time." He rummaged through a kitchen drawer stuffed with old bills and canceled checks. "Here."

The girl needed no more prompting. Fortifying herself with assurance, she tore a piece of notepaper from a pad and scribbled with the pen. Placing the canceled check next to the paper, she leaned forward, fixing her eyes on the signature. Gliding the pen over the paper, she practiced a few times. Then she turned. "Quit staring at me," she grimaced.

"It looks pretty good," he said.

Her attitude hadn't altered. "Maybe you should do something else," she protested. "I need to concentrate."

He agreed, and after a few more moments of watching went out.

CHAPTER 11

SIKES WAS PUTTING on his newly acquired boots when the boy entered the men's room. There was someone in one of the stalls. The man put his fingers to his lips. The toilet flushed as Yoshi stepped into a vacant stall and shut the door. A lanky fellow wearing a dusting of powdered sugar on his t-shirt walked over to the basin. He washed his hands and then grinned into his reflection and picked some food from his teeth. "Mighty nice they provide donuts at these things," he said. Yoshi heard Sikes agree. "If it weren't for the donuts, I don't think anyone would have stayed. To tell you the truth," the speaker said, "I can't stand these booktalks, but the coffee keeps me coming back!" There was a rustling of paper towels right before the door opened and closed.

"You can come out now." Yoshi poked his head out. "Think I could come by your house. I could get some more of that soap. Just about all used up."

The boy stammered for a moment before answering. "Sure, it's just right now my mom is still kind of sick. I can bring it back here if you want."

"When."

"When?"

Sikes zipped up his backpack and stood up. "Yeah, when?"

"Day after tomorrow."

"That would be Wednesday." He pulled the spiral pad from his back pocket and thumbed through the pages. "Mid-morning works for me." He flipped the pages over.

"Sure, I can be here."

"Good. Say 10:30?" He smoothed his hair with his palms and then ran the water while he wiped the basin with a piece of toweling. "See you then," he exclaimed and pitching the towel into the garbage strolled out.

Yoshi stood in the men's room, wondering if they had anymore bar soap. His mind flitted as he reconstructed the bathroom closet. He was feeling guilty about his snap decision not to have Sikes go to the house. Surely, he wouldn't be offended by a later offer. He would apologize for his rudeness and explain that he didn't want any of his mother's germs to get him sick. Yoshi was sweating. He pulled a piece of toweling from the rack and wiped his face. He needed to get home and see how the girl was managing, much of their future was riding on her.

Go look, stupid. It was checked out. *Maybe it was returned. Not everyone reads as slow as you do.* He detoured to the bookshelves. "See, it's not there."

"What's not there?" A grim-faced librarian was squatting down as she pulled books from her rolling cart.

"*The Bell Jar,*" he said.

"Did you look in the Ps?" she asked.

"It was checked out."

She didn't answer and went about her business in a gloomy mood.

When Yoshi arrived home, the girl was still at the kitchen table. A half-dozen balled up pieces of paper were sitting in a dirty breakfast bowl. "I got it," she said, looking up from a flattened sheet of paper. "See."

"You're a genius," he said.

"I know." She handed him the paper, and he grinned.

She's not ready. The Colony needs to know. "We should throw these away," he said.

"Duh!" It was evident she was insulted.

"I know you knew that."

She gathered the balled-up evidence and threw it into the trash. "Let me know when you need my skills."

"Where're you going?"

"To read, what about you?"

He shrugged his shoulders, but he lied. He knew exactly where he was going.

He sensed there was someone else in the cellar. "How'd you get in?" Frito was leaning against the railing at the bottom of the steps. He pointed to the window. "You jumped down?"

"Of course not." The visitor pointed to the short ladder. "Ivan found it in the corner and pulled it under the window for me."

Yoshi nodded but didn't remember any ladder. He yanked on the cord hanging from the ceiling. The yellowing bulb offered a stingy bit of light to the room. Kojo was sitting on the lawn chair. "Don't worry, you won't have to creep back up through the window when you leave." He was the only one that laughed.

"We saw you with that guy today." Hawk stepped out from around the washing machine.

"Sikes?"

"Yeah, what happened to his eye. He looks like a boxer."

The three of them sat down on the floor in a circle under the bulb, all except Kojo, who liked his position on the chair.

"I don't know." *I didn't notice his eye either.*

"Well, between the glass eye and the tattoo, he might be a boxer," said Hawk.

What tattoo? I didn't see a tattoo. "Tattoo? Are you sure we're talking about the same guy?" Yoshi joined the circle next to Kojo.

"Yeah, he came out of the men's room right before you." Frito nodded, confirming that he was also there.

"Why didn't you say something?"

"Cause I could see you had everything under control. I think he looks like one too." Frito smiled at the proposition of a real boxer.

The idea that he hadn't noticed a glass eye made the boy's head hurt. *Don't you remember stupid? Think, think.*

"Actually, we're here to tell you that we have to be more careful with our notes. We're going to have to write in code." Frito leaned back and pulled a folded piece of paper from his pocket and handed it to Yoshi. "This tells you how to write and crack the code. It's pretty easy to follow."

"If I can do it, anyone can," explained Ivan. The small boy's cheek had turned a yellowish-green, less bruised than the last time he saw him.

Yoshi started to unfold the paper but was abruptly stopped. Frito pushed his hand forward, preventing him from looking at the information. "Not here, you can do that later. Right now, we need to know if you're on track."

"Nothing will stop me," he promised.

"Good, but don't tell us anything else. We can't know how you're going to do it."

The boy nodded.

That boxer guy could come in handy," Kojo added.

"In what way?"

Hawk rolled his eyes. "Are you sure you know what you're doing?"

"Rule number 3, Everything said and done is kept a secret," reminded Kojo. "Sikes the boxer may be able to help you keep what happens a secret. Not that he will know anything. His unknowns are your secrets."

They all smiled except Yoshi. He was still trying to make sense of it all.

* * *

SIKES ARRIVED AS a stranger and was still a stranger. The Colony tried to help but succeeded in only adding more questions and offered no answers as to how to handle a boxer. The street-sleeper could be a boxer, he had all the markings of one. He had a glass eye, it took nerve to steal the bag… on the other hand, he did give up half of the money. Maybe they were wrong. Maybe he was a Robin Hood kind of boxer, one with a conscience. For the latter reason, Yoshi acquiesced to his own belief of the stranger. With the instructions in his pocket, he and the rest of The Colony were able to transmit messages confidentially. But there was still the missing ingredient. How was he going to take care of his problem?

This was a silent moment. Yoshi sighed deeply when he was accosted by a frightful voice. Shouting down the stairwell, Henrietta stood at the top of the rickety steps and holding firmly on to the banister so as not to fall face first. "What the hell are you doing down there? Get up here!"

Taking two steps at a time, the boy dashed up. "I was checking on soap. Laundry soap." He lied. "What's wrong?"

"Why should anything be wrong?" she asked. She looked fragile except for her eyes. They always looked piercing. A flat-faced man with straw-like hair stood next to her. "This is Edmond," she said. "He needs to stay here for the night. I told him he could sleep in your room."

"My room?"

"That's right; show him where it is while I get a cigarette." She walked into the kitchen.

"Thanks, kid; I wouldn't have asked, but nothin' else came through." The boy turned his face away with a start. The odor that came out of the mouth smelled rancid.

"What 's going on?" asked the girl.

"Edmond is sleeping in my room tonight."

"Your room?"

Yoshi nodded, however, when he went to open the door, Henrietta appeared directly behind Edmond and pulled him aside. She whispered something in his ear. He nodded and then followed her to the back door. She handed him a small paper bag, gave him a peck on the cheek, and pocketed the money he handed to her. "Never mind," she said to Yoshi. Her cigarette butt was leaving a trail of grey powder as it fell freely onto the floor.

"He's not staying here?" the girl asked.

"Other arrangements were made," said the mother. "Do me a favor, put this in the jar, and buy yourselves Chinese for supper."

"Do you want any?"

There was a thoughtful pause. "Egg rolls and a pack of cigarettes. Tell the guy there's a good tip in it if he brings me some cigarettes."

"Cigarettes and egg rolls, that's easy," said the girl. But the woman did not detect the sarcasm as she went into the bathroom.

Yoshi covered his face with his hands. "That was a close call," he moaned. He uncovered his face and pinched his nose. "A stinking roreg ledling in my room."

"It wouldn't have happened."

"Why not?"

"Remember what I put under your bed. You don't have to worry." It had been a long time since the girl's eyes looked so bright.

"You're so ulti!"

"I know," she agreed. "But, we need to get more lemons," she said. "Just in case, be sure to lock your door tonight."

We can pick most locks. But don't worry, you're one of us. He stared fixedly into her eyes like a squirrel about to be run over.

"What's the matter?"

He pointed to Henrietta's room. "We gotta talk."

"We always talk."

"But this is different." He started for the cellar door, but she ignored him. "It's the end of our lives as we know it," he said.

Saachi smiled deviously. "Not today, I hope."

"You don't believe me." He opened the door leading to the basement. "Come on." For a moment, she watched as her brother ambled down the stairs. There was a voice in his head, but he didn't listen. He didn't want anything to distract him. The ladder was still under the window. He smiled quietly to himself. "This is going to be a wonderful day."

"Why stooky down here?" she asked as she bounded down the stairs. She brought her annoyance with her.

"A keytret."

"What kind of a keytret?" She sat down in the lawn chair while he leaned against the wall.

"One that can never be spoken outside this room."

She smirked at his answer, but his silence lay thick in the mood he was in. "You're serious, aren't you."

"Yoyu."

"Does it have something to do with Mrs. Willy?"

"Mrs. Willy?"

"She still hasn't come back from the hospital." She bit her lip.

"So."

"So, it's my fault. I buried the lemons and salt in her yard."

Her answer caught him off guard. For an instant, he agreed. "Even if it was, she probably deserved what she got." He watched the girl's expression lighten.

"I suppose you're right," she said as the moment of uncertainty passed. "Well, what is the keytret about that's got us down here?"

His eyes flicked over his sister. "Remember when I said we had an egmol? Well, we can get rid of it for good."

"For good like forever or just a little while."

"Both. We can start with a little while and see how we feel. If we like it, then forever." There was something in the way she stared that made him understand they were more than connected in thoughts, secret thoughts. One could not get along without the other. "Henrietta is a tobler and roreg. But she is also dactie. It's only a matter of time before she's caught, and then we'll be separated."

"Separated." Her statement did not come as a question. "By who?" This was a question.

"The pop-pop."

"Nocoo, I won't go."

"They won't give us a choice." He sounded sincerely correct.

"Shit." She wanted to smash his head in, she didn't want to hear any more.

"Alyo flitloy de Henrietta!" he said. The girl was carefully decoding his words. His was a remarkably good idea.

"Get rid of Henrietta," she repeated. He nodded. There was very little else for her to think about except to agree. "That seems reasonable," she decided.

"Want to go up and have a soda."

"Sounds good!" she exclaimed, and leaping out of the chair shouted, "last one up is a rotten egg!"

The pounding of feet on the stairs echoed behind the boy as he followed his sister. The day had turned out to be almost magical, it had been a very good day indeed.

CHAPTER 12

NOTHING SHOCKS THE young, much less a street-sleeper. He was in the eyes of the boy a super-tramp, although the word tramp never entered his vernacular. Sikes was a man of originality. His rough exterior did not vanish when he was around the boy, and that is what made him trustworthy. Thoughts of the future were as distant as the stars, and the past was a deep as a black hole. A metaphor that offers more than enough fodder for the imagination, Sikes's history was not terribly unique nor tragic. He was by most accounts cunning. Why he was cunning was not because he was clever, it was because he was lazy. He had a strong dislike for labor. He had been acquainted with drink at an early age although had an aversion to strong tasting liquors. Begging was a fine art that was relegated to those who had mastered the originality required to be successful, a skill he left for the most learned of beggars. He went about his life in a dogged way, more spider-like than fly-like.

He had been traveling for several months when he arrived at the library. After a short rest, he would continue westward, where the land was big and the climate warmer. Those were his intentions until he met the boy. The youth did not care that he was washing his feet in the sink, this was a sign of one of two things, either good upbringing or very lousy upbringing. Their first encounter lasted less than fifteen minutes, long enough to produce a bond and short enough to produce a scheme. Life is funny that way, we take the good with the bad and hope for the best.

Whether it was because he was hungry, wet, or if someone saw him mattered not. Sikes knocked on the front door. It was late, and there was no answer. So, he snuck around and tried the back door. This time a hand slipped the curtains aside. "There's a guy outside on the stoop."

Yoshi got up. "Who's there?"

"Sikes."

The girl sat back down and continued to eat her egg roll as Yoshi unlocked and opened the door. A man grinned cheerfully. "I would have phoned first but didn't have your number." He took a whiff and smiled greedily. "Chinese?"

Saachi showed little restraint. "There's not enough to share," she said.

"He can have some of mine." Yoshi stepped aside and let him in.

"Thanks, kid."

Water dripped from his backpack and off his clothes. "You're wet," she said, glaring at the intruder.

"It's raining."

"You're making a puddle."

"It's only water," the boy retorted and turned to Sikes. "You can sit down, but Henrietta is sick." He lied.

"She's always sick," said the girl.

"Nothing contagious, I hope."

"No, nothing you haven't gotten a few times."

Yoshi scowled at his sister.

"I'll go on downstairs and change," the intruder suggested. "I know where everything is."

Saachi looked wide-eyed as the man excused himself and headed into the cellar. In less than a minute, he came back up with just his pants on. "Mind if I pull the mattress away from the wall. I'm pretty tired."

"What's that?" the girl asked.

"This?" he said.

"What's it supposed to be."

He lowered his chin and looked down at his chest. "A dream catcher."

"What's it mean?"

"It catches bad dreams."

"And then what?"

Sikes shrugged his shoulder. "Hides them until they're crushed into stardust."

She contemplated his answer. "Okay, want an egg roll?"

"No thanks, I already had one."

* * *

HE COULDN'T SLEEP. He heard Henrietta try to open his door around midnight. Light from the hallway floated under the door as Yoshi peeked over his blanket and then shut his eyes tight. She twisted the doorknob but couldn't get in. She tried again. He wondered if she did that all the time. He could hear several voices in the living room. A woman laughing, and then a shhhhhh. A man with a strange accent was talking low. Then everyone started to laugh. Yoshi listened and waited for several minutes until he got out of bed. He felt a reckless need to find out what was going on. He cracked open the door wide enough for him to slip out into the hall and crouched down so he couldn't be seen. There were four in the living room with their backs to him. The streetlight provided the only light in the room. Interest was centered upon the preparations being made by the man with the accent. He lifted the lid of a black lacquered box lined in silk, similar to a jewelry case. It contained parts of a wooden pipe and a tiny brass bowl he removed and began to assemble. He handed it to Henrietta while he opened the box to retrieve a small spatula. He dipped the spatula into a thick, gummy substance but was suddenly stopped.

"Not here." She stood up, and all but the man with the box followed. Yoshi scurried back to his room. The anticipation of being caught was more frightening than if Henrietta actually saw him. He pulled the door closed, turned the lock, and scrambled into bed. But no sooner had he lifted the covers over his head than did he race back and place his ear flat against the door. "Don't be afraid. Inhale, but very gently," Henrietta said.

"Blow through your nostrils. You know how to smoke." A high-pitched voice added impatience to the instructions.

Yoshi couldn't tell who they were talking to. Maybe it was a new lady gryphon. It didn't matter to him who it was and decided to go back to bed when he heard Henrietta say. "Well then, maybe we should go to the cellar."

"Cellar?" Her words stoked panic, rousing an immediate instinct to warn Sikes. What if she finds him? *Shut up stupid, you're freaking out!* But she'll suspect something. *Suspect what. Some guy that looks like a boxer sleeping on a dirty mattress. Just shut up and listen!* And he did.

"The cellar?" The high-pitched voice rose an octave.

"I'm only kidding, come on, we can all fit in here."

"Good, I hate cellars and basements."

"Aren't they the same thing?"

The boy could hear the last pair of feet shuffling behind a chorus of snickering and jokes as Henrietta escorted them into her room. "We always fit," the woman said. A giggle and then a sultry "oh stop that!" sailed out as the bedroom door closed.

Yoshi sat with his back leaning against the door. His head was resting on his crossed arms, supported by his knees. He glanced up at the clock and yawned. "Lemons," he thought. Tomorrow he would be sure to get some lemons. He wanted to go to the bathroom, but he didn't dare go out.

* * *

THE MOTHER HAD no recollection of the accident when she woke up. Clearly, there had been one because her foot was bandaged, and bloodstain prints led from the hallway into the bedroom. She held her hand against her heel and then limped to her dressing table. She looked into the mirror with the same sensation as a person having slept in a different bed. "What happened?" Her search for some truth stopped short; there was nothing in her brain to refresh her memory except a sloppily applied bandage. She turned away from the mirror and stumbled back into bed. She tossed the sheet over her. "Who the hell are you?" It was too dark to see; she couldn't be sure. Did she even go into the cellar? Why did she want to go into the cellar? She never went down there. Her hand hurt. It was cut. How did that happen? Was I alone? "Maybe I'll remember in the morning," she thought and closed her eyes. But it was morning.

"I met your mother last night."

"My mother?"

"You're right, she's sick." Sikes was sitting in the chair. He had pulled the mattress back up against the wall.

"What happened?"

"As far as I can tell, she stumbled over a few things. In the streetlight, she saw someone, me, sleeping on the mattress."

"There's blood on the floor upstairs."

"She broke a bottle of wine. A real shame dropping a perfectly full bottle too." He pointed to under the stairwell.

"You're cut!"

"Yeah, she was pretty f'd up."

"It's okay, you can swear. How'd you get cut?"

"She came at me with the broken bottle. Luckily, she only scratched my arm when I pushed her off. I'm surprised you didn't hear her." Yoshi's head ached. He wanted to talk to The Colony. Everything was getting screwed up. "She won't remember anything," Sikes said. "They never do."

They? They, what does he know? The echo laughed in his head, and the boy clenched his fist until it stopped.

"What's for breakfast?"

Get him out of here. "You want breakfast?"

"Aren't you hungry when you get up?"

"Yeah, but I just thought…"

"Thought what?"

Thought what, thought what! He's hungry stupid. "Nothing. Cereal. I can bring some down."

"What kind?"

"I think the store brand like Corn Flakes only sweeter."

"Anything else?"

"Bread. We have bread."

"I'll take the cereal. Actually, forget it; I better go."

"You don't have to go if you don't want to." There was no point in being disappointed, he wouldn't have blamed Sikes for leaving and never coming back.

"Mind if I take this?" It was a t-shirt. Yoshi shook his head no. "One more thing, I can sell some more of that stuff that was in the paper bag." He was slouching in the lawn chair quite content, as though he were amused by his situation. A monstrous wave of noise rushed into the boy's head. He didn't hear what the man said. All he saw were lips moving, followed by a crooked smile. Then the noise poured out of his ear canals, and they were clear. "If you want," Sikes continued, "bla bla bla…"

Yoshi agreed.

He leaned over and pulled his spiral pad from his back pocket and thumbed through several pages. "I'll come back in a few days to pick it up." The cellar window was swung open. Yoshi waited for Sikes to get up and move the ladder into place, but instead, he saw the street-sleeper ooze out of the chair like a serpent and crawl on his stomach out the window.

* * *

"I'VE BEEN GLAPPED."

"By who?"

"Sikes."

"What kind of a glap?"

"A taken-for-a-fool kind of glap. I thought he was different." The sorrowful remorse did not offer the girl a convincing explanation.

"Different from what?"

"He's a roreg too."

"That sucks."

"He wants me to give him the paper bags."

"Do we get the cabbu?" she asked.

"We can split it."

She cocked her head to the side with an expression of interest. "I have to go to the dragon's. We have no more lemons."

"Okay. I have to think."

"What about her?" she asked. "I saw some blood on the carpet and dirty bandages.

"I wouldn't worry about Henrietta. She cut her foot on a broken wine bottle."

"Where."

"It's in the cellar."

The girl sighed. "I'm not sure there are enough lemons in the world to help us."

* * *

IF HENRIETTA HAD wanted, she could have killed Sikes. The boy knew where the gun was kept; in a shoebox on the top shelf in the garden. He pulled *The Bell Jar* off the library shelf and held it securely before skimming the pages. It was like meeting up with a friend that you haven't seen for a long time. The note was wedged into the center pages. Just as expected, it was coded.

W*atchooutoforotheomanoinoyourobasementoflushowhenoyouoareofinishedoreadingo*. Only the signature line was left decoded: Frito. He folded the page in his pocket and sat down at a table. Several pencils and pieces of paper were set out for patrons. The instructions to break the code were easy. A dummy letter o had been placed between each word. W*atch-o-out-o-for-o-the-o-man-o-in-o-your-o-basement-o-flush-o-when-o-you-o-are-o-finished-o-reading-o*.

It wasn't a very cryptic note, more like a fortune cookie. He would flush it later; he didn't feel like doing it now. He had just slipped the paper into his pocket when he felt someone tap him on the shoulder, "Isn't it time you went home?" Gustave pulled a chair out for himself and sat down. "How's it going, Yoshi?"

After the stress of the night and morning, he was relieved to see someone from The Colony. "I'm okay, what about you?"

"No problems. *The Bell Jar* is back on the shelf."

"I know, I got the note."

"And?"

"And I will."

"Good." Gustave drummed the table. A lapse between moments of conversation can feel like an enormous gap. He seemed to be waiting, as if he knew there was something on Yoshi's mind. There was.

The boy spoke up. "Do you think some people are more like a machine?"

"In what way?"

"Going about the day without thinking, as if they were on automatic."

"Like an automaton?"

"Like a soulless person."

"That would depend on two things; if you thought they had a soul in the first place and if your definition of being human includes having a soul."

"Let's say to be a human, you have to have a soul."

"Like a ghost thing floating around or more like a conscience like thing?"

"More like a ghost-conscience," Yoshi said.

"I guess so. Never really thought much about it."

An idea was slowly forming in Yoshi's mind, and as he looked across at his friend, he told himself he was no longer confused. "If I'm right, then it will be much easier to come up with a permanent solution."

Gustave appeared less troubled by Yoshi's philosophical quest for answers. "Soul-less, heart-less, however, you want to justify your decision on how to solve your problem. Call it any way you see fit."

"How'd you fix your problem?"

Gustave smiled. "It was easy, I just had to wait until my big brother made my Dad go away. One afternoon I got home from school, and everything was all cleaned up."

Yoshi nodded with envy. He wished he could push it off on someone else. "I gotta get home," he said. He stood up and put his hand in his pocket. He hoped Gustave couldn't tell the note was still there.

"See ya, Yoshi."

"See ya, Gustave. And thanks." A silent field of positive energy fell over his space, and as he walked, he could almost feel himself float. He turned to wave goodbye, but the sunlight coming into the library window was too bright, and it blinded him. But it wouldn't have mattered much, Gustave was gone.

CHAPTER 13

"WHAT'S THAT?" SAACHI looked down at the plate the dragon had finished preparing.

"Lunch."

She leaned over and took a sniff. "Smells like fish."

"It is. Would you like a taste?"

"I'm not a big fan of fish."

"This is different. It's raw."

"Raw?" Her scowled face displayed nothing but displeasure at the mere thought of uncooked fish.

"It's a Japanese delicacy that, if prepared incorrectly, will kill you."

"Oh, then give me a big old piece!" she exclaimed with sarcasm. The dragon did not laugh. "Seriously?"

"Quite, but have no fear. I am a master chef and have no intention of killing myself nor you." He was stony serious.

"What kind of fish is it?"

"Fugu."

"I'm having a tuna sandwich when I go home. So, I don't want too much fish in one day." He nodded with understanding; she lied not to hurt his feelings. "I only came by for some lemons."

"Look in the basket," he said. "Take as many as you need." He stood at the kitchen counter, and using a pair of chopsticks, plucked the fish from his plate into his mouth with one delicate motion. The girl followed his directions and picked out three lemons from a pile of assorted citrus.

"Can I have these?"

"Certainly. And how are your seeds doing? They are fast-growing once they get started."

"Yoshi is taking care of the plants for me. They have lots of leaves already."

The dragon smiled with his eyes. "I'm pleased you are using the lemons and salt."

"Me too. I think it's working."

He chewed, slowly finishing each morsel with great enjoyment. "There is no reason they wouldn't," he explained. "I have many old recipes if you need others."

"I wear this all the time!" she announced and pulled the leather amulet up from under her shirt.

"Are you sure you don't want this last piece," he asked.

"Very."

"Is there anything else?"

"Nope, thanks for the lemon!"

"You're welcome. Do you need a bag for those?"

"I can carry them okay. Maybe I'll try your fish another day."

"Anytime, I like to eat it at least once a week."

* * *

"ONCE A WEEK!"

"Yes, and he said if it wasn't prepared correctly, it would kill you."

"What kind of fish?"

"Fopi, or fugu, or oh, I'm not sure. All I know is that he eats it raw with sticks."

"Did you taste it?" Yoshi wanted to know what it was like.

"No way."

"I think it sounds cool."

"Then you go eat it."

"Maybe I will."

* * *

WHEN IT CAME to privacy, there were not many places in a house a boy could go to. The basement had become his refuge, but even this room had become crowded at times. The window leading in, once stiff from lack of wear, was now easily breached.

Gustave was the member of The Colony that was sitting in the lawn chair when Yoshi turned on the light. "Twice in one day!" he said.

"I hope the code wasn't too hard to understand," Frito asked. He looked different; he had a haircut too short for his ears.

"It was fine. Did Gustave tell you we met."

"That's why we're all here."

"You don't mind, do you?" Hawk asked. "The window was open."

"Well, everyone, but Ivan, he had a little trouble," explained Kojo.

"What kind of trouble?"

"He was caught smoking a cigarette. Ironic, isn't it? His grandmother grounded him. So you see, Yoshi, maybe you don't have it so bad after all."

Yoshi joined the circle of boys sitting on the floor. "Gustave told us what you talked about, and now we can see you're on the verge of great things."

"Great might be a bit of an overstatement," Yoshi said.

"Great is a mental state."

"Then I don't feel very great, more curious."

"About what?"

"Well, now that you're all here, maybe you can tell me if anyone has ever heard of poison fish."

"Called?" asked Hawk.

"I think yogu or fugu or,"

"Or you don't know."

The boy felt stupid. "I better look it up."

"Only thing that swims that freaks me out is a giant squid," said Gustave peering down from the lawn chair.

"Oh, yea, a giant squid!" laughed Frito.

"I hate fish. Every time I have to eat fish, I want to puke," Kojo said.

"What about tuna?" Gustave challenged.

"That doesn't count, it comes in a can."

"I hate all fish, canned or not," Kojo contended. "I'm a meat-eater."

Such a statement each boy could agree on, except for Frito, who admitted it was kind of expensive to buy unless it was Spam. Here there was a consensus of agreement, except for Hawk, who didn't know what Spam was. "I'll be right back; we have a can upstairs."

Yoshi had no intentions of opening the can when he returned, the picture on the outside would be proof enough that it really was meat in a tin (with other stuff mixed in). "I can't believe you never ate Spam," protested Yoshi as he bounded down the stairs.

"But I have."

"Sikes!"

"Who'd you think was down here?" The street-sleeper had just entered and was standing under the open window. Yoshi felt hopelessly vulnerable as he looked from The Colony to the man, back and forth his eyes trialed both.

"Don't worry about us," explained Frito. "We'll just wait here until he leaves."

"You sure?"

"Am I sure about what?" Sikes asked. He took several steps further into the room when Yoshi stepped back.

"Does he want something?" asked Gustave.

"I'm not sure he wasn't supposed to be here until a few days."

"Who the hell are you talking to?"

"Us!" piped in Frito. "Got a problem with that?"

"Yeah, got a problem with that?" Hawk echoed.

"Well," asked Sikes, waiting for an answer.

"Them," said Yoshi pointing to The Colony.

Yoshi moved further towards the circle, the can of Spam still in his hands. He leaned over and gave it to Hawk. "These are my friends."

The can of Spam dropped to the floor. Sikes rubbed his stubbled chin with a half-cocked expression of confusion. "Come back later, after we're gone," explained Frito. But the man didn't move.

"I think Frito is right, maybe you should come back later. We're having a club meeting," Yoshi suggested

"Maybe tomorrow," said Gustave added. He pulled himself up taller in the lawn chair.

There was a strange look that had come over the man's face. The boy appeared to be fine, yet he wasn't. "I'll come back to get the bags day after tomorrow."

"Okay." The Colony applauded, and Yoshi smiled. They watched as the glass-eyed boxer pulled the ladder over, skip every other rung, and then creep out the window.

"Now," said Gustave, "where were we."

"Spam," Hawk said, reading the label. "You were telling me about Spam."

* * *

FATE HAD WILLED that the kitten's short life be ended before it was full grown. The girl picked up a stick and poked the bloated stomach. It had all the markings of having suffered considerably before taking its final breath. "It's eept," she said. The tiny animal's mouth was open and contorted. A foamy layer of saliva covered its muzzle and tongue.

The boy bent over and looked inside the jaw. "It must have eaten something bad," he said. He stood up and pointed to the garbage can. "Out of that."

The girl nodded. "Poison guts." Pieces of raw fish were scattered near the dead kitten.

"We better tell the dragon."

"He's not home; I saw him go out."

"Then we need to have a funeral."

"Do we have a box?"

"Wait here," he said.

She knelt down and blew her hot breath over the animal. Then she poked it a little more with the stick. "Yep, you're dead," she told the kitten with dissatisfaction. It was a cute cat, but stupid, she decided. "It wasn't a very smart idea to eat out of the garbage," she scolded. "Besides, now it stinks." She turned her nose up at the remnants of trash that had been indiscriminately tossed about. The boy quickly returned without a word and set the shoebox down next to the carcass. He pulled from his back pocket a spatula. "What's that for?"

"You don't want to desecrate the body, do you?" he asked and inching the blunt edge under the cat as if he were going to flip a pancake, he lifted gently and released it to the empty box.

"So much for not wanting desecration! You dropped it!" She shoved the boy aside and looked in. The kitten was very stiff. "Did you bring a pillow?" She smiled and then laughed. It was a nervous laugh, one that had an undercurrent of stress.

Yoshi lifted the box. "We can dig a hole in the backyard."

"Or throw it in the furnace."

"I never thought of that," he said. "But I think a grave might be more traditional." A pecking noise at the window attracted his attention, and he saw a crow sitting on the outside ledge and shooed it away. "We better get this into the ground."

Saachi carried the trowel to the back fence where the ground lay bare from any grass. "If we just stick it in the ground without the box, we won't need such a big hole," she decided after scrapping several heaps of earth to the side. "Here, it's your turn."

Yoshi handed her the box to hold. He found the area chosen less than optimum for the ground was hard and pocked with small stones. After several minutes he stood up, and they admired their work. "Maybe a little deeper," he said and proceeded to stab the sides of the hole with more vigor. "We don't want a dog to dig it back up," he announced. It appeared that the hole was getting wider instead of deeper.

"Let me at it," she protested, grabbing the trowel from the boy. After several more scoops, a careful inspection confirmed it was ready for burial.

They stood side-by-side, their eyes fixed on the empty grave just in front of them. "Do you want me to start?" he asked.

She nodded, yes. The boy knelt down with the open box and slowly rolled the kitten into the hole. It fit rather snuggly, except for the tail that took a bit of maneuvering. Then they took turns pouring the dirt over the little animal, and after several pats with the flat plated side of the trowel, it was firmly planted.

"Poor kitten, I hope it rests in peace," said the girl.

"Me too."

They stood for several minutes, neither in the mood to say anything. It was their first funeral, and it opened up a world of unknowns.

The dragon heard them as they approached the side of the house. He was sitting on the porch with the mother cat on his lap. He stood up and leaned over the railing, still holding the cat in his arms. "Lemonade?"

The girl nodded yes and without waiting for the boy, skipped ahead. "Come on," she said, turning to her brother. The dragon had already entered the house.

"I think I'm going to put our stuff away; you can go in without me."

"Suit yer self."

He turned and walked back down the steps as the screen door opened and then slammed shut. A husky voice instructed Saachi to the kitchen, and the pouring of liquid over ice with the tinkling of the cat's bell followed.

But Yoshi didn't go home as he had intended. His thoughts were on the buried kitten. If there was one dead kitten, then there could be more. Statistically, it didn't seem probable that its siblings were dead, especially since a cat is supposed to have nine lives. As he retraced his steps back to the garbage cans, he wondered if Saachi was telling the dragon what had happened. There was a distinctly foul odor coming from the open can. Its lid had been tipped aside and a crevice large enough for a small cat to get in and out of omitted the stink. *Go on, don't be a baby, look inside!* He tried to hold his breath without pinching his nose. *Take some out, take some out!* A balled-up piece of newspaper had been unraveled by the cat and lay on the bottom of the can. Aside from some cut up pieces of flesh and fins, all the other organ parts looked like a pile of brown mush. Yoshi lay the pail on its side and slid the paper out. Then he rolled it up and returned the pail upright, securing the top. A few flies had already started to congregate in search for any fish remains but would be disappointed. Yoshi was in possession of what had been gutted. A seamlessly solid and timely plan, all he needed to do was hide the pieces in the freezer for later.

There was a note taped to the back door. It must have been placed after he had gone home for the trowel. "Washing machine" was all it said. It had been written in a hurry. The door had been left unlocked when they went out, and he now wondered if anyone had gone inside. The kitchen was in the same unkempt state that they left it, used plates, and toast crumbs on the table with juice glasses stacked up in the sink. He listened for signs of life as he tiptoed to the refrigerator and opened the freezer door. He moved the ice trays and pushed the balled-up newspaper to the back. It was a small space, but since there were only the ice trays and a freezer-burned package of spinach, he expected no one would look inside or, better yet, care.

He followed the note down the cellar steps when a dramatic change of expression fell over him. The room that he had mentally dubbed his own was occupied by Henrietta and an unfamiliar man. The two didn't hear the boy as he stopped in the middle of the stairway. Their voices raised in simultaneous laughter over something they both agreed was humorous. "Come on, Arp, I think we got it all well placed." Slowly, the boy backed up the stairs and stood by the cellar door. Arp was talking, but his voice was too garbled to understand. Then there was laughter again and the sound of feet producing lazy strides up the stairs. Yoshi ran into his room before they could reach the top of the landing, quite sure his presence had not been detected. He shuddered with silent gratitude that he had not been caught. The note was still in his pocket, and he mentally read it aloud. "Washing machine." Whatever roogs Henrietta had hidden was most likely not in the washing machine, or so he hoped.

It wasn't the knock on his door that woke him. It was the girl's annoyed voice. "What happened to you?" She looked down and saw the peacefulness that had been on his face turn sour.

"When?"

"I thought you were coming back to the dragon's, I waited."

"Sorry." He sat up. "I must have been ladling."

"Henrietta went out with that roreg."

"Arp."

"Yeah, how'd you know."

"They were in the cellar hiding roogs. I accidentally saw them, but they didn't know I was there." He had a pessimistic feeling that he didn't want to talk about. It was better when he was asleep.

"I told the dragon about the kitten."

"What did he say."

"He said it was good that we buried it." She sat at the edge of the bed as if tending to the sick and sighed with the passion of an old soul.

"I need to go to the cellar." He pulled the note from his pocket and handed it to her. "This was taped to the back door."

"Who put it there; that weirdo, Sikes?"

He suddenly felt a lump in his throat, the kind that swells when there's dread. *They didn't see him, don't be such a chicken!* He swallowed. "Maybe."

"Washing machine?" she shook her head. "He's so dactie."

"You don't like him, do you."

"Sikes, why should I?"

Yeah, why should she? "No reason. I'm going down to the cellar."

"Here," she said and pulled the amulet from around her neck. "You might need it."

"No thanks."

"Then I'm going with you." She slipped the necklace back on and followed.

He imagined the cellar and its dimly lit light and Sikes sitting in the lawn chair wearing just his boxers. His boots neatly set beside his bare feet. But there wasn't anyone downstairs. The girl lifted the washing machine lid and looked in and then stepped aside. "There are clothes in here." The boy dipped his hand in and lifted a pair of men's pants. "I think he wants me to do his wash." She turned and removed the detergent from off the shelf and poured some onto the dirty clothes. "I thought you didn't like him."

"I don't." She set the machine to on and set the lid back down. There was an immediate sound of water rushing. "Is he a witwit?"

"I'm not sure. I didn't think so.

"He stole the bag, so he must be."

"But he gave me half the money."

She pondered his answer for a moment. "So he glapped you."

Now he pondered the question. *Yea, you idiot, you were tricked!* His head ached, and the noise of the washing machine was growing louder. "Let's go upstairs." *That's right; go upstairs and don't face your troubles.* He liked Sikes, and that was his problem, not because he had been deceived, but because he had believed in something that could not be. He wanted Sikes to be someone he was not. *You're running out of time, stupid.* His sister's footsteps on the creaking steps traipsed behind. There was a wicked smile on his face as he turned around; "I have an idea." They reached the landing, and the door slowly closed behind.

CHAPTER 14

"THERE ARE OTHERS like us," Frito said. But Yoshi didn't need reminding. "I don't think we should see each other until you're finished."

"What about Saachi?" Gustave added, with a bit of suspicion.

"I'm going to tell her later. She knows I have an idea."

"And Sikes?" Hawk asked.

"He knows nothing."

"That's good." Frito's face brightened. "We all need a fall guy."

"Fall guy?" the boy at first didn't follow.

"You know, a fall guy, somebody who might take the blame." Kojo was quick to clarify.

Yoshi nodded with understanding. "Fall guy," he repeated. Yoshi didn't ask how The Colony had gotten into his room. He was just happy to see them. All except Ivan, who was still grounded, they were all there, all sitting on the floor in a circle. It was all quite remarkable; he saw himself in their eyes as if he were looking at himself.

"How's your father?" Hawk asked.

"You know I don't have one," the boy remarked. There was a tick tick tick sound from the clock that crept around the room like a small animal.

"You'll be able to breath better when it's all over," Kojo said.

"One last thing. Don't destroy the garden. You may need it." Frito stood up, and the rest followed. "Well, good luck, amigo."

Yoshi opened the bedroom door and stuck his head out. He gestured for the others that the coast was clear. He watched anxiously as the last boy sprinted through the hallway and out the back door, all except Frito, who limped as fast as he could. He went back in and remained for some time sitting alone in the dark. So far, he had succeeded but was now on his own. He took a pad from his desk drawer and started to make a list. Henrietta, Sikes….. He stared at the two names and then crossed them out. He didn't need a list, it was all up here, in his brain. Everything he needed had been actualized. Keeping a list would only mean keeping evidence; such a stupid idea. *Yeah, that was a really lame idea making a list.* It was a scream so loud in his head that he ripped the sheet from the pad and tore it up into tiny minced pieces. *Flush it!* He clenched the bits of paper in his palm and snuck into the bathroom. The toilet gladly accepted his gift, and as he watched, it sucked the confetti into its gullet. He felt like he might vomit.

✷ ✷ ✷

"WHERE THE HELL is the aspirin?" A plea for help rang out from the bathroom. The woman stormed into the kitchen; her head was enormous.

"Isn't it in the medicine cabinet?"

"If it were, would I be standing here in my nightgown?"

Yes. Yoshi didn't answer.

"Where's your sister?"

"Reading."

The mother pulled the chair away from the table and slinked down like a snake. She folded her arms and rested her head on her bare arms. "What time is it? Is it still morning?" She lifted her head and then held it in her hands.

"Maybe you're hungry."

"Bla bla bla bla," he heard her sulk.

"Okay, then maybe I can make you lunch, later."

"Blaaa blaaa blaaa…!" He watched her mouth get inordinately round as she spoke. He hoped her head wouldn't get any bigger.

"I don't know, I thought it might be nice."

She gave a small nod of approval and offered a glint of a smile. "Call me when it's ready then." Her face was powdered with makeup, and her lipstick was smeared above and below the lip line. Even so, there was a slight change of expression, as if she had become human. It was her voice, it wasn't angry. She snatched a pack of cigarettes off the counter and stumbled out.

He didn't think she would, but now that she accepted, it was time. He had to work fast. His breath grew short, and his heart began to pound. *What is your problem?* "None," he told himself. *Good, now think, what do you have to do first?'* "Take the scraps out of the freezer." *That's right. So, get off your butt and do it."*

Three sitting at the table for lunch, it would be like a family meal. He picked the tuna out of the can and dumped it into a glass bowl. The unwrapped newspaper was in the microwave set on high. After a few seconds, he took it out and poked around to make sure it was thawed. He parceled out the meatiest pieces and tossed them into the bowl. *Smells like a bait shop!* "I'm not done!" He stared into the refrigerator. There was an old jar of pickle relish and mayonnaise on the side racks. He searched for another thing he could add, but the refrigerator was more like a temporary resting place for old food. The celery was blanch and rubbery, and the lettuce resembled cooked spinach. He left them in the vegetable bin, where they didn't bother anyone. After adding a few scoops of mayonnaise and relish, he mixed everything together around with a fork; to his amazement, it was beginning to look good. There was still some bread left in the loaf, enough to make a tuna sandwich for Henrietta and peanut butter sandwiches for himself and Saachi.

He ran his hand over the table and tossed the crumbs to one side and placed a pack of napkins over a grease spot. Then he poured three glasses of water and set them before each place setting. "Lunch is ready!" He looked at the oven clock, 11:45. He hovered by his seat and after a moment, tried again. "Hey everybody, lunch!"

Saachi entered the room saying nothing and then took a sip from her water glass. "What's the occasion, so fancy?" She eyed the boy cunningly. "Is she coming?"

His eyes looked back like two blue marbles. "Yoyu."

"Maybe she went back to ledli." They waited. "Let me try, I have a better voice for this. Lunchtime!" she shouted.

It was now 11:49. "Maybe she's yarmied."

But she wasn't, she was cross. "What the hell are you two shouting for?" She stumbled into the kitchen dressed in a pink satin bathrobe and barefoot. Her eyes met the table and began to soften.

"Lunchtime," the girl said.

"I made you a tuna fish sandwich with relish."

The girl looked impressed. "I want that too." She sat down and picked up her sandwich. "Peanut butter? How come I can't have tuna?"

Yoshi turned to his sister and opened his eyes wide. "There isn't enough for you." But the girl didn't understand his look and continued to sulk.

"Here," said Henrietta. "You can have half of mine," and with an unusual gesture of compassion offered her sandwich.

The boy gasped like a goldfish out of its bowl. "No," he snapped at his sister. "I made this special for you, I put your favorite on your sandwich. Grape jelly!"

The girl pushed her finger down on her bread and let a bit of jelly ooze free. Their eyes met, and for a brief instant, it was as if she understood.

"Are you sure?" Henrietta asked. Her face appeared cadaverous, the skin stretched taut except for the sunken cheeks, and the dark eyes set deep into the eye socket.

"She's sure."

They both watched as the mother took a bite of her sandwich and started to chew. Her jaw moved back and forth until she finally swallowed. The food moved along her throat like a boa constrictor, the small lump working its way down until she smacked her lips. "What did you put in this, it has something chewy in it. Maybe rubbery."

"Chewy?" he said. "Nothing chewy, just relish." She took a heartier bite and chewed more slowly, trying to discern what the texture was. "Maybe it was a little bit of the celery," he said.

She swallowed and then nodded her head. "It could be the celery."

"Do you like it?" the girl asked, not the least bit envious that she didn't have tuna fish.

"It's different," the mother added. She was reluctant to eat anymore; however, Yoshi fixed his eyes on her until she took another bite.

The kitchen had become strangely normal with a regularity about it that was almost agreeable. The boy lowered his eyes to his plate, every so often tossing a glance in the direction of Henrietta, who had managed to ignore the unusual tastes of her sandwich in exchange for civility. Yoshi suddenly realized the power of the child over the parent. But such control is short-lived, and when she was finished, she pushed her plate to the center of the table and asked for her cigarettes and a toothpick.

"Do you want any more?" he asked. His thoughts went to the garbage pail and then to the fish guts and wondered what she would say if she knew what he had added to the tuna. *There are others like you.* Frito's mantra buzzed around in his head.

Her thin fingers wrapped around the cigarette as she struck the match and held the butt to her lips. She blew the flame out. "No, I've had enough." She slouched in the chair and smoked. "I'm going to a party tonight, so I won't be home." She tapped the cigarette ash onto her plate. "Did you water the plants?"

"Yes."

"Good."

The girl sat at the table moodily. "Can we order Italian later?"

The mother twisted her neck and head; the rest of her body remained completely stationary. "Pizza?"

"No, Italian. Maybe garlic bread and pasta."

"Sure, take some money from the jar. And be sure to tip the guy." She inhaled deeply and then crushed the cigarette out on her plate while the smoke exited her nostrils. She unwound herself and stood up. "I'm going to take a nap, so be sure to play quietly."

The boy looked at his sister and shrugged. He couldn't remember the last time anyone told them to play quietly. Henrietta picked up the pack of cigarettes and started to walk to her room when she stopped and turned. "We should do this again sometime." The figure of their mother then retreated behind the closed door.

He felt the room sigh with relief when she was gone. He got up and began to scrape the leftover tuna fish into the garbage. He ran the hot water and filled the empty bowl with water setting it into the sink.

"You did it, didn't you?"

"Yep."

"And you're not joking, are you."

"Nope. But we must be sure not to tell a soul. This is a keytret. A very onder keytret."

"That, brother dear, is an understatement."

* * *

AFTER SHE CLOSED the door, she slipped off her robe and fell into bed. The sunlight shone under the blinds, and she cussed at its intrusion with her usual candor. She pulled her pillow over her head. She hadn't counted on falling asleep so quickly. But a minute or so after drifting off, she was woken by a tingling on her lips and a burning sensation in her mouth. She squinted, and in the darkness, she saw startling splotches of light. *How each child deals with their existence is fate.* But she couldn't think about that now, she was too busy trying not to vomit. She pulled herself up, quivering to the bathroom. She leaned over the toilet and heaved so hard that she saw her stomach fall out of her mouth. *You've vetoed everything.* But she couldn't think about that either, she was too busy trying not to fall. She was sick, a kind of sick she needed to be in bed for. The taste of tuna fish lingered in her mouth and on her breath. The only way to get back to her room was with help, but she couldn't get the words to move above her Adam's apple. They were stacking up like a glob of peanut butter stuck to the sides. She had to ambush her trapped self and pry herself away. Her legs were making stiff bird-like movements while her extremities twitched. The afternoon was feeling like a thousand miles long. She dragged herself slowly out of the bathroom and into her room. "I can't move my legs! Help me! Help me!" A ring of words rolled out of her mouth and traveled down her cheek into a pool of saliva. And then, she felt cold, tomb cold. There was no life left in her extremities, they were numb. Only a glassy stare from her cat-like pupils remained.

"She looks like a fish out of water," said the boy.

"What's she doing now?"

"Just lying on the floor."

"Maybe you should put a blanket over her."

"You think she's cold?"

"No, eept."

"I'll check." The boy opened the bedroom door and peeked in. He knelt down and poked the mother with his finger and then touched her arm. *What are you looking for?* "I don't know," he said to himself. He held his hand on her back and then pulled back when shallow breaths of air moved her bony body up and then down. "Don't worry, Mother." He didn't know why he said that; it just seemed like something you were supposed to say.

The girl walked into the room and pulled the blanket from the bed. "Her feet look weird." She handed him the blanket. "Put it over her legs too." He did. But the most startling thing about the woman was her face. The head was turned to one side and flattened against the floor like slices of white bologna. "Maybe she wants to see herself." Saachi took the pink plastic hand mirror off the dressing table and tilted it. The mother's face took up most of the glassy surface with a deadpan stare. "Look! I think she blinked." The girl kept the mirror still as Yoshi leaned closer.

"I think she's a zombie," he whispered. "Yeah, a real zombie!"

Saachi tossed the mirror on the bed and stood up. "Don't be dexif, there's no such thing."

"I'm serious! She's got that vacant glare."

The girl got on her knees and bent down eye level with the woman. Then she stood up. "If she's a zombie, I don't think she's going anywhere. "

The boy leaned over and spoke in a low, soothing voice, "I'm going to water the plants now."

"Now?" parroted the girl.

"Yea, want to come?"

"What about her?" she asked. They both hung their heads, looking over the mother.

"How are you, Mother?" He spoke loud and slowly. "We'll be back to see you later." A great weight had been lifted off his shoulders. A rumbling of voices in his head was distant like the sound you hear when you put the opening of a conch shell to your ear.

The girl stepped around the woman and trailed the boy out into the hall. "That was a really good peanut butter sandwich you made."

"Thanks," he said. He felt good, it was nice to be appreciated. He led her to the garden door, where the lock had not been secured. "Careless of Henrietta," he said, pulling it free from its latch. There was a smell of fertilizer and damp soil rising from the beds, almost toxic. It was an unnatural place, where plants grew out of enormous troughs filled with dark soil. Designed by the woman who too sequestered herself inside the house, its presence yielded foliage neither for beauty or sustenance. The girl meandered over to where she had planted her seeds. They had grown tall with fingerlike leaves fanning over younger shoots. She gently stroked the leaves as if they were wings from a bird. As for Yoshi, he was investigating a newly constructed planter wedged against the back wall that had been partially filled with topsoil and flattened with a brick. An ungainly stack of unopened bags of soil leaned awkwardly against the side walls.

"What would happen if we mixed these leaves in with the others?" Saachi picked one off and brought it over to her brother.

He put it to his nose. "I'm not sure. I guess after they're dry, no one would notice." There was a wickedness in the girl. "You can pick some now and lay them on the drying trays with the others. Arp will never see the difference. He's just a dactie gryphon."

She walked back to the planter and started to pinch off the leaves. "I don't think it matters if some tear," she said. The boy went over to the new planter and leaned in. "I know what you're thinking," taunted the girl. She had finished lining all her plucked leaves side-by-side on the tray and pushed it into the drying rack before shutting the closet door. "It stinks in there," she exclaimed and leaning all her weight against the wall, tipped her shoes forward.

"How do you know what I'm thinking?" he asked.

"Because there can't be anything else on our minds." She dropped back down on her flat feet and then up again.

"Are you finished?"

"I think so."

"Good." He walked around the room and pushed his finger into the soil of each planter. "They don't need water today. Overwatering is even worse than dry." He spoke with authority.

"Will you check on the leaves next time you water?"

"Sure."

"Do you think Henrietta liked these plants?"

He locked the door behind them and turned. "No, she liked the other roogs she buys. This is business. Being a gardener." They both laughed.

When Yoshi opened the bedroom door, the mother was still lying on the floor; only her foot was sticking out from beneath the blanket. He walked around the room and picked the pillow up from the floor, and placed it flat against the headboard. Frito was standing in the doorway and smiled. The boy felt calm and amid the circumstances, happy to see his friend. "I'm glad you're here," he said.

"I hope I'm not bothering you, but I couldn't wait."

"I understand," Yoshi said. All his anxieties had now been condensed into a single moment, this one. He turned on the lamp. Henrietta's mouth was open, but no sounds were coming out. Only a puddle of minced letters, which had dropped from her lips, was scattered like dust around her head. "I think she tried to say something." He turned to where Frito had been standing. The threshold was empty. Only a dark hallway occupied the space. A sliver of sunlight was shining between the blinds, and with it were small pieces of dust floating in the light. At first glance, they drifted in random directions until he made an extraordinary observation, it wasn't particles of dirt but individual letters forming a tiny word. It said Eept. The boy pulled the blanket back over the bare foot. He was feeling hungry and wondered if Saachi was in the mood for spaghetti. "If anyone comes for you, I'll let them know you're resting. We're ordering Italian. I don't suppose you want any." Her face was immobile, and soon the blood would drain away, leaving her very pale. He could see a few pin curls pulling her hair back away from her forehead. "Don't worry, we'll keep this our family keytret just the way you like things." Then he left and closed the door.

They decided that the office chair in the living room would work. All they had to do was get her up into the seat and push her to the kitchen table. "When Arp comes by to take her to the party, we'll only let him look in and see she's not feeling good enough to go out."

"Why don't we just put her back in bed?"

"Cause if she's in the chair, we can move her around."

"Until she's really eept."

The boy nodded. "We're not the only ones that do this. There's others like us."

"I know you said that already."

Yea, she's not stupid. His head was beginning to hurt.

"I don't know what kind of seeds I planted."

"I thought the dragon gave them to you."

"The ones in the garden were my choosing."

"You mean you're a witwit."

"Nocoo, he said I could take some, so I did. I just forgot to ask him." She slipped a pink sweater off the chair and put it on. "I'm going next door."

He had an awful impulse to laugh. They were going about the day as if it were ordinary, so matter of fact while Henrietta lay in the next room paralyzed. He wondered if they would ever miss her. The girl hadn't bothered to put her feet into the sneakers and slipped them on with her heels mashing down the backs. She slid across the floor as she waved goodbye and trundled down the back steps when, in a matter of only a few moments, she returned. She was accompanied by Sikes, who had apparently been traipsing up the walkway as she was leaving. The girl opened the door and let the street-sleeper enter. The boy was thrown off guard and plainly showed his displeasure as Saachi started back down. "Don't be too loud cause Henrietta doesn't feel well," she cried over her shoulder as either a warning or a reminder.

"Your sister doesn't like me, does she?" Sikes asked.

"She just doesn't know you."

"I didn't want to come in through the cellar window; the last time was a disaster." He was referring to the encounter in the dark with the woman. "You look surprised to see me," he pointed out, drawing his disappointment of the boy with his expression.

He's testing you stupid, act casual. The boy smiled and tried to appear pleased to see him. "Come on in and sit down. Are you hungry? I think we have some leftovers."

"What kind of leftovers?"

"An egg roll."

"That would be nice." He shut the door behind him and pulled a chair from the kitchen table. "Smells like fish."

Shit, he knows! "We had tuna fish, but it's all gone. He picked up the bowl from out of the sink and held it up."

"What's wrong with your mother?"

"I think it was something she ate." He offered the remaining egg roll still in the white paper box and put it before the man.

Sikes nodded, tore open the lid, and dipped his fingers into the container. In two bites, he had dispatched his meal. "I love leftovers." Then he pulled a toothpick out of his top pocket and began to nudge the tip between his gums and teeth. "They say it's as good as brushing." When he was finished, he wiped the tip on his shirt and slipped it back. "Do you think I could use the bathroom?" His glass eye stayed in one position while the good eyeball rolled toward the hallway.

Yoshi remembered the last time he let the man use the bathroom. *Go ahead, let him. You'll need this guy.* He felt his head begin to throb. *Be nice.* "Sure."

Sikes produced his backpack that he had shoved under the chair and got up and started to walk into the hallway when Frito appeared. "Just want to be sure you're okay."

"I'm okay."

Sikes had not gone too far when he turned quickly around. "Were you talking to me?"

Frito laughed and touched Yoshi on the arm. "Tell him to mind his own friggin' business."

"I can't do that," he whispered. "No, I didn't say anything." The boy pointed in the direction of the bathroom, "you better hurry, my mother might need to go in."

"Sure, kid."

What seemed like forever was only about ten minutes. "I feel a lot better," Sikes said, stroking his chin. The boy looked nervously around the kitchen as the cleanly shaven man came out from the bathroom and stood behind the kitchen chair. "You'll need to take out a new bar of soap. I took the one in there."

"That's good," the boy said. He tried to look indifferent and pushed a few dirty plates to the center of the table.

Sikes pulled his pad from his back pocket and thumbed through several pages. "Got a pencil, I just want to jot down when you think I can come back for the paper bag."

"How'd ya know I didn't have it now?"

"You would have mentioned it to me."

"I'm not sure, maybe in a week."

"A week!" He was obviously annoyed.

"My mother's sick," Yoshi reminded him.

"You wouldn't be lying to me, would you?" The words entered Yoshi's ears and got stuck in his throat. His eyes widened as Sikes made an insolent smirk. The remark seemed to have given the boy what he needed to clear his throat.

"I don't lie to friends," he said and handed him a pencil. "I can meet you at the library, in the men's room. Next week."

"You're a great kid, Yoshi." He picked up his backpack and dropped the pencil on the table. "I won't forget."

The image of Sikes washing his feet in the sink flashed before his eyes. He tipped his eyes to the wall clock, becoming suddenly aware of the ticking in his head, and he wished the man would finally leave. Sikes turned the doorknob. "Bla bla bla bla," he said and sauntered out.

It was eerily quiet after the man left. Even the clock's ticking had died away. Yoshi went into the living room and slipped behind the curtain. He slid down on the floor and pulled his knees into his chest. The smell of fish was still on his hands. *Go to the mountains. Go to the highest one you can find.* And so, he did.

CHAPTER 15

"**H**OW CAN SUCH a thin person weigh so much?" They each had taken one side and tried to lift her into the chair, but it kept rolling out from under her. "Wedge it against the bed," the boy was weary and losing his patience.

"She's not eept yet, I think she has no intention of eepting at all," the girl complained and letting go of her grip the woman collapsed back to the floor. Thin and rigidly jointed, her contour stood out under the folds of her nightgown with the stiffness of iron pipes.

"We have to do this," he explained. "She can't stay here forever." Memories and remorse should have been surging up within the children now, but they weren't, and each paused over the body and gazed as if into murky water.

"We seem to have an onder egmol. She's getting kind of stiff. Mother, can you just bend your legs a little?" Saachi asked in her very sweetest voice. "Ugh, why don't we just roll her?"

The idea seemed for the moment quite good until the width of the door squashed that idea. "I know, if we put her face down on the chair seat and her arms folded along the back, we will at least have half of her weight distributed on the chair. All we have to do is have one of us keep her steady while the other pulls from the front."

"And where are we wheeling her? I thought you wanted Arp to see her sitting when he came to the door. It would look kind of weird if she looked like she fell asleep with her head on the chair seat."

He hated when she was sarcastic. 'Nocoo, we move to plan B. We'll just tell him that she's sick in bed."

"And…"

"And, we'll gonna take her into the garden."

It was his menacing look that provoked her will to try again. She made no reply, and picking up the woman's arms pulled hard. "She looks like a store mannequin," she exclaimed cringing. "This is creepy." The mother dipped at the waist, her legs drawn out straight, and her hair fell over her face.

"One more onder shove, and we'll have her up!" and calling attention to their progress, the boy wheeled the chair in front of the ragdoll mother. "You hold the chair while I pull." And seizing the wrists, he began to pull upward while Saachi turned her head away as she steadied the chair. "Don't get soft on me now!"

"I'm not, it's just that she's staring at me! Tell her to close her eyes!" And suddenly, the absurdity of her decree provoked a shrill of laughter.

"Why would she listen to me now!" howled the boy.

The mere idea sent the two into hysterics until finally, when they had succeeded with their mission, the mother's upper body and head were folded over the chair with the pale legs stretched behind. Her drooping arms flopped over the chair, and the fingernails like claws of a bird tipped the floor. Yoshi raised his thumb up as they started the procession. He pulled from the front, and Saachi steered from alongside, gingerly they extracted her from the bedroom. After exchanging a few compliments, the woman's head began to grow larger, and Yoshi began to worry that if it got too big, it might not fit through the doorframe. He glanced over his shoulder and stopped. They hadn't counted on anyone coming to the house. He put his finger to his lips. A loud knock at the front door and a woman's voice called from outside. A look of panic fell over the girl as her mind flitted.

"Quick, let's put her in the bathroom," Yoshi whispered.

"The bathroom?"

Again there was a hurried rapping, and this time the calling from two different voices. "We don't have time to open the garden lock. Hurry up!" With little effort, they were able to wheel the mother into the bathroom, parking her in front of the toilet. Pulling a bath towel off the rack, Saachi draped it over the woman's head and torso. "What's that for?" he asked.

"Privacy."

It was a tight fit, but they managed to turn the chair and pull the door shut.

Two women were waiting outside on the front steps when Saachi looked out the window. "It's Henrietta's toblers."

"Let's get it over with," Yoshi said and unbolted the lock.

A lanky woman with cropped hair backed down a step when the door was open. She began to talk in a low voice as if she had something in her mouth. "We're here to see your Mom."

"Both of us," added the blonde. She was wearing a rumpled skirt that matched her eyeshadow, purple.

"She's not here."

"She said she would be, what time is it?"

"Does it matter?" chanted the girl.

"She had to go see a sick friend and won't be back today." He lied.

"When will she be?" quizzed the taller visitor.

"In a day unless that guy dies. Then it will take longer for her to get back," Saachi explained.

"Dies!" The blonde shuddered.

"He's really sick. Henrietta thought it might be contagious," Yoshi added studying the two women as a sudden change of expressions forced their faces to sour.

They appeared noticeably uncomfortable. "Do you think we know who it is?" whispered the dumpy blonde and tugged at her friend's sleeve. "Okay then, I guess we'll go. When you talk to your mother, tell her we were here."

"Oh, we'll tell her as soon as we see her!" mocked Saachi.

"Let her know we have it all, she'll know what we mean," the tall woman mumbled. A blatant display of disappointment was gestured as they both sulked down the walkway.

"Do you want to tell Henrietta, or should I?" teased Saachi as she shut the door behind her. She ran over to the window and pulled aside the curtain. "They got into their car and are just sitting there. Now the little one is looking in the mirror and putting on lipstick."

"Did they leave yet?"

"Now, she's moving the mirror around. Okay, now they're pulling away from the curb." A moment passed until Saachi stepped away. "Let's go tell Henrietta," she said, but Yoshi had already come up with the same idea and was timidly opening the bathroom door.

"Hello Mother, two of your toblers came to buy roogs. But we sent them away so they wouldn't bother you. We've come to take you to the garden." He inched the door open and lifted the towel away. Her head had deflated and was resting comfortably on the seat. "Saachi, can you squeeze in and push her from behind?"

"I think so," and with one hand balanced on the door, she nimbly tried to get around the legs. "You gotta push her towards you, or I'll be in the toilet! There's no room ya know!"

Hurry up, stupid! His head was beginning to throb. He had become the guardian of the family honor after the natural laws of nature were broken. There was nothing else he could do. Humanity had become forgetful, all construction built between parent and child had toppled. Perhaps now they could get some peace; all he wanted to do was sleep.

It wasn't a very difficult job. The newly laid blanket of black soil had been packed down hard and being as she was not a big woman, with legs slightly bent she fit with enough room for slippers. The girl insisted she be buried with her pink slippers. The only challenge was getting her into the planter, however, after they figured out how to flop her over the side, head-first, their options became obvious.

"I'm tired, can't we finish tomorrow?"

"I suppose it would be alright," he said. The mother didn't appear to be uncomfortable.

"I'll cover her with her blanket for tonight." Her suggestion seemed perfectly reasonable, and she smiled. "Then, we can order dinner."

"Tomorrow you can go to the bank and cash a check. We'll need some money, just in case."

"In case of what?"

"Just, in case."

She agreed and felt very content, knowing she was the one who would be responsible for getting money. "Goodnight, Henrietta. I'll be right back to tuck you in!"

"Tuck you in?" questioned the boy.

"That's what I read. Sometimes when someone goes to bed, another person tucks them in."

The boy raised his eyes as if he were star gazing and then lowered them. "We could try it, but we'll have to take turns."

"Alright," She smiled. "We could try it."

"And the one doing the tucking will be the one to turn off the lights."

"We can leave a nightlight on in the hall, just in case one of us gets up in the middle of the night. To go to the bathroom or something." Her voice quivered slightly.

"Okay," he said. "I think that's a very good idea."

* * *

IN HIS MIND, thoughts scattered like a trail of crumbs and were immediately plucked away by a flock of unruly ideas. He and the girl were like wild horses that should have been broken. "Mother, what do you see when you look at me?" A handful of soil poured from his hands. At this rate, it would take hours. "You might take a while to disappear. The house is full of your steps." He lifted the bag of soil and dumped it.

"How many bags will it take?" Kojo asked.

"Probably all of them."

"I think you're right."

"I'm glad you're here," the boy said. He lugged another bag from the closet and split it open. The earth seemed friendly in his hands, but slightly damp.

"Need some help?"

"No, I got it." He scooped some more out and sprinkled it in. He turned to Kojo and smiled. Kojo nodded. He understood. There was little to reconcile as he filled the trough and packed it down gently with the brick leaving enough room for future planting.

"You're a victim that became a predator. We all are," Kojo said.

"I guess I am," he admitted cheerfully. He stood with his hands on his hips, admiring his accomplishment, staring at the planter. But he didn't look too deeply, he didn't want to breach the surface.

"If you don't need me, I think I'll go."

"There are others like us, aren't there?" Yoshi said, but when he turned around, he was the only one in the garden.

When Saachi returned, she placed the money in the jar and waited. She crossed her legs and leaned comfortably in the wingback chair. She needed a new book to read. She'd ask the dragon, he had good taste in books. "Maybe now I can invite my friends," she thought. Her mind drifted to all the things she'd have to say. "Oh, my Mom, she's visiting her sister. Henrietta, she hasn't been feeling well." All very probable reasons for the woman's absence. No one asked before, so why would they care now? "Oh, my Mom, she's working late."

"I didn't hear you come home," the boy said as he rounded the chair and plopped down on the sofa.

"You're dirty!" she exclaimed.

He looked down at his hands and wiped them on his pants. "I was putting her to rest."

"You're all done?"

"Yea, well almost. We just need to decide what to plant."

"I guess we need to do something now."

"Like what?" He was too tired to do anything else.

"Aren't we supposed to say something, like other people do over a grave?"

"It's not a grave, it's a planter."

"Yea, you're right. I guess we could put a marker in and write Henrietta on it." She laughed.

"They do name roses after people, so it's not so farfetched." There was a twinkle in his eye when he said it. "I'm going in to take a bath. When I get out, we can order dinner. Anything you want."

"Italian?"

"Okay, with extra garlic rolls."

He stood up and smiled. The girl looked at peace. *The vultures will be gathering soon. You need a plan.* He was getting a headache. "I'll have one by the end of the week." *Why so long, think, think!* But he couldn't think, he was just a kid trying to survive. *Stop feeling sorry for yourself. There're others like you.* He walked into the bathroom and leaned over the side of the tub. He turned the faucet on full blast. A thunder of water shot out of the spigot. *There was an old lady that swallowed a fly, I don't know why she swallowed a fly, perhaps she'll die. There was an old lady that swallowed a fly, I don't know why she swallowed a fly, perhaps she'll die.* The ditty was flowing out and filled up the tub, over and over it sang when finally, the tub was full, and the water was turned off. The twinge in his temples subsided, and the last few drops of water sang from the faucet, *dead, dead, dead.*

CHAPTER 16

"**W**HY DO YOU go underground like a mole?" the dragon called out from his perch. He moved slowly across the front porch and looked down over the railing.

With a bruised cheek and dirt-stained knees, the stranger presented himself. "I'm a friend of Yoshi, he always lets me in."

"Yes, I know. I've seen you on several occasions." The dragon was drinking a glass of lemonade and paused to put his glass down on the small table beside his rocker. "Why not go through the door like most other guests?" There was no sarcasm in his voice, but rather remarkably non-judgmental considering the facts at hand.

"His mother is sick."

The neighbor weighed the information and nodded. "She is sick often. Still, the cellar window seems more trouble than it's worth unless, of course, you have other intentions."

"Such as?"

"Keeping your presence unnoticed. Catlike perhaps. They are very good at coming and going unnoticed." He watched Sikes move from the side to the front steps. "No," he thought, "he's more like a fox than a cat."

"I'm Sikes," he said.

"I know," remarked the dragon. "I don't suppose you'd like something to eat. I was just preparing my favorite dish when I heard you pass by. Do you like sushi?"

"If it's not too much trouble. I never pass up free food."

"Good, then why don't you have a seat and I'll put some together for you. It's too nice a day to be inside, don't you think?" The dragon's billowy white pants caught the breeze, and he looked more like a man sailing than walking. The spirit of the day had lifted for the hungry man. He had been caught in the rain and slipped, his cheek scraped on a rock as he toppled to his knees, dirtying his pants. It was a comedy of errors. He had hoped to exchange his clothes for others, taking a few unused belongings out of the cardboard box in the kid's basement when he was caught. "Shitty luck." However, he was beginning to absolve the day for starting out lousy now that he was going to get some food.

His stomach was an empty hole waiting to be filled, the skill is the ability to train it to wait. Each man owns his own misery; his was refilling his stomach. Through the screen door, there were sounds of chopping on a cutting board, a noise meant to soothe his whining stomach. He imagined the strange man working meticulously, mincing tender pieces of fish and rolling them up in seaweed and rice. An uncouth boor he was not, rather he liked to think of himself as a traveling vagabond. A man of mystery roaming the world. "Well, maybe not the world," he thought, "more like a modern-day hobo riding the transit system." Somehow his mental description had lost the romanticism he had intended.

"I think you'll find your meal to your liking," the dragon explained. "There's a dipping sauce in the bag as well as a pair of chopsticks." He dangled the sack in front of the seated man like a dog with a bone, but before it could be snatched it up, it was delivered with a warning. "Next time, go to the door. I wouldn't want Henrietta to mistake you for an intruder."

"She's still sick, I thought."

"She still has a gun, I know."

Sikes coughed just at the moment of interpreting this bit of information, preventing him from accidentally saying something stupid. The man before him was deadly serious and equally still. "I guess I'll be going. Thanks for the sushi!"

"I am sure you'll enjoy it, some have told me, 'it's to die for.'"

"That good, huh?" quipped Sikes.

"Indeed."

The dragon picked up his lemonade and sat back in his rocking chair. He could hear the cats outside trolling the garbage cans. He turned his eyes down and examined the cut on his finger. "A rather clumsy thing to do," he sighed.

Sikes walked away and followed the broken sidewalk like a man who had just found a dollar in his pocket he didn't know he had. "Maybe my luck is changing," he rejoiced. A woman walking in the opposite direction turned down a street as he approached. "What's the matter," he called after her, "never seen a bum before?" The woman twisted her head and then scurried along as not to draw attention to herself. "Well, I'm not a bum," he shouted, "I'm a ..." Sikes stood in the middle of the sidewalk and stroked his stubbled chin. "What the hell am I," he thought. "Hungry," he decided, "I'm just plain hungry." The woman had disappeared from view, yet he continued to stare into the distance. The houses along the streets became blurred, and he wiped his eyes with his sleeve. The edge of the sidewalk may have been the end of the earth. He dipped his foot off the pavement and pressed it into the grass. "An improvement over mud," he said, placing his foot back on the sidewalk. He pulled his pad from his back pocket and ran his finger along the front page. Then he flipped the cover over and shoved it away. Neither annoyed nor embarrassed by the disquieting event, which seemed to have evaporated, he continued on his way.

The librarian looked with blatant irritation before answering the boy. "I imagine the entire library collection would be consumed."

"That's what I thought," he said.

Suddenly the woman's mouth contorted as if she were expelling an enormous yawn. "Such a dreadful question. What would make you think of such a thing? A fire, of all the ideas." She remained steadfast at her post, her hands resting on the desk, ready to check out a book. To the boy, it didn't seem like such an outlandish idea. With all this paper, accidents can happen. "Is there anything else you wanted to ask?" Her tone was exasperated but not angry.

"I don't think so." He moved away from the librarian and sat in one of the over-sized chairs. Such a nice big room and so much silence. There were all kinds of silence, he decided. Church silence, in your head silence, moment of silence, deadly silence; he was experiencing library silence. There was no reason to go to *The Bell Jar*, there would be plenty of time for that. A man with bulging eyes and mottled cheeks was sitting several chairs away. A book on his lap lay open to the same page for quite some time while his lips mouthed something across the room.

He said you're the son of a dog murderer. "I can see." *But did you hear what he said? He's an asshole. Get up and ask him what he's reading.* The boy shuffled over to the man, who now had lifted the book up to his face with the title facing outward. *Lord of the Flies.*

"Ever read this?" asked the dull man feeling the presence of the boy.

"I prefer *The Bell Jar*."

"Isn't that a bit old for you?" His eyes squinted when he talked.

See, I told you he was an asshole. "Not really."

The man smiled. "Don't forget your belongings." He pointed to the two bags under the chair.

"I won't." The man drew his eyes back to his book. Yoshi walked around to the back of the chair and glanced over the reader's shoulder. "We did everything adults would do. What went wrong?"

In the memorial garden, the primroses were blooming. It was a bit of a surprise since they were not flowering the last time Sikes was there. With a muttered remark about the boy being late, he reached into the bag and fumbled with the aluminum foil. Wasting no time with chopsticks, he fingered the sushi and ate several pieces. Then, not giving his mouth time to savor the exotic taste, he gobbled two more. He wiped his mouth on his sleeve and sighed contently. It would be easy to finish them all, but he decided it would be more prudent to save the last piece for later.

The boy was carrying two paper bags, one large and the other small. He appeared eager as he opened the glass doors finding the scenery inviting. "The air out here smells different," he remarked.

"It's the flowers, they're in bloom." Sikes pointed behind him without moving his head. "And the sun is out. Altogether it's a pretty nice day." He tossed a glance in the direction of the parcels. "One of those for me?"

"Actually, both." He set the grocery bag in front of the bench and handed the smaller one to Sikes. "I brought you a sandwich." He looked down and noticed the folded piece of aluminum foil.

"Your neighbor gave me something to eat?"

"The dragon?"

"He didn't say his name. He told me your mother has a gun."

"She only uses it on dogs." Yoshi sat down. "Then I guess you're not hungry."

The man opened the bag and pulled out a sandwich secured in wax paper. He put it to his nose. "Tuna?"

Yoshi nodded. "I made it myself."

The man thought about the woman on the sidewalk and then thought of the boy. "A small bit of kindness can fill an entire stomach," he said and unfolded the wax paper. The smell of fish accompanied his gesture. "Must be fresh," he grinned.

"Very," said the boy.

"Want half?"

"I already ate." He got up and walked over to a bed of unnamed plants. They were not particularly pretty, rather more ordinary. A few were beginning to open their buds, some with variegated leaves, others marked by ragged edges.

"I bet your mother likes your cooking, this is very different. It almost has a chewy texture."

"She didn't complain if that's what you mean." The boy returned to the bench and sat next to the man. "It's my secret ingredient." He watched as Sikes licked his fingers and then refolded the paper and slipped it into his backpack.

"I taped this closed," Yoshi said and pushed the grocery bag with his foot. "I didn't want it to open up when I was walking over."

"That was a good idea." He closed his eyes and lifted his face to the heavens. "I'll be by later to bring you your half of the money." He kept his eyes closed when he spoke.

He watched the man for several minutes. "I need to get home," Yoshi explained.

"I haven't had fish in ages and now, twice in one day, and in the same meal," he laughed. "Funny, isn't it."

"Must be your lucky day," said the boy.

Another patron pushed open the glass door as Yoshi slid past. The man made himself comfortable and sat down on the opposing bench from Sikes. "Nice afternoon to sit outside," the fellow said. "This is a charming little oasis," he added, and propping his duffle bag next to him began to make himself right at home. With a conscious eye on the door, he mapped out the garden, a habit he had developed with time. He glanced over at the figure sitting on the bench, which now moved like a bird preening itself. However, who was he to react to the eccentricities of others and decided to watch the birds instead.

Sikes opened his shirt and swatted his throat. He was sure stinging gnats were swarming on his face and neck. A tingling on his lips made him quiver while extremities stiffened. Helpless horror confronted him as the realization set in, he had been manipulated by a wolf pup. Sikes sat motionless like a temple frieze, his head drawn back, and his feet planted apart. All his weight relied on his knees, abandoning any other means of support.

"Are you drunk?" asked the patron who had opened a thermos and poured a cupful of black coffee. "I could give you some of this. It might make you feel better." But the only utterance that came from Sikes was a low moan. The coffee drinker, a man who was of little means, for he was wearing clothes that were too large and too sooty for a gentleman, eyed the backpack and paper sack. However, the strap was wrapped around the seated man's shoulder while the sack remained virtually abandoned. The boy watched from the inside through the glass doors as the paper bag was nudged away from the bench. Sikes, unable to retrieve his belongings, did the only thing he could physically manage, he snorted. "Don't worry friend, I'm just going to see what you have in this bag." A fitful whimpering that should have been heard coming from the ill man was ignored as a yellow poncho was pulled from the bag and held up. Examining it like a fish, he turned it over and then stretched it out, and did the most unlikely thing. He rested it upon the shoulders of the seated man. "It's of no use to me," explained the other. "I have a plastic bag I am quite fond of. I do hope you feel better. You look a bit under the weather."

The man folded the bag and set it back where he found it and sat down across on the opposite bench. "I don't suppose you have a cigarette?" he called out. The snorts and guttural noises that escaped from Sikes were taken as a negative answer. "Better you don't smoke," said the tramp and screwed the cup back on the thermos. He pulled up his pants and tightened his belt. "I will leave you to your peace," and exited through the garden gate.

A sparrow, barely the size of a fist, fluttered near the bench. It hopped from seat to seat, looking for something to eat. Taking a bold move, it neared the feet of Sikes and then hopped up upon his knee, and although it weighed not more than a few ounces, it was just enough disturbance to alter the balance of nature. As if in slow motion, Sikes toppled over on to his side and then rolled from the bench to the ground. No one heard him fall; this was deadly silence.

The boy turned to Frito, and they walked together to the bookshelf. Yoshi pulled *The Bell Jar* from the shelf and opened it. Then he leafed the pages and closed the book. "I was sure there would be something for us," he said with disappointment.

"And from who do you think?" Frito asked.

"Maybe Henrietta."

Frito took the book from Yoshi and placed it back on the shelf. "Give her time," he said. The librarian walked up from behind, pushing a cart. "If you're not taking a book from here, I'll just ask you to move aside for a moment, so I can shelve these."

"No, we don't mind, do we?"

"We?" the librarian remarked, frowning. "Are you trying to be insolent, young man? There is no we, I was simply asking you to step aside."

Yoshi looked at Frito and shrugged his shoulders. "There are others like us you know." The librarian gave him a frosted look and proceeded to find room for Patterson on the upper shelf. He stood for a few moments and watched as her arms and hands grew longer and longer until they were able to reach the highest shelf. She fit the books snuggly together and started to roll the cart away. "You better check on the guy in the garden," he called out. "I think he fell asleep."

She stopped in front of the Rs and ran her hand across the spine of the books. "Better he sleeps out there than in here," she remarked.

"She's right," whispered Frito. "Better there than in here."

CHAPTER 17

"SHUT YOUR EYES."

"How come?"

"Just shut them." Her voice demanded he do as she asked. "Don't peek!" There was a quick scurrying around and then, "Okay, now look!"

He opened his eyes. "What do you think?" She was wearing Henrietta's pearl necklace, earrings, and a rhinestone tiara.

"Fancy," he whistled.

"I know, I always wanted to try them on, and now I can." She paraded around the room, her feet slipping out of the silver high heels. "She's got a lot of stuff we didn't even know she had."

"Like what?"

"Like a box of jewelry, some perfume, pocketbook with money, and roogs."

"We'll give the roogs to Arp. You can write a note in her handwriting and tell him to get rid of them." He thought for a moment. "We'll tell him that the pop-pop came by and threatened her."

"Do you think he'll believe it?"

"It doesn't matter. We have the black book. He's got to split the caboo with us. If not, we'll get some other gryphon to do it."

"How come I have to do all the work?" she moaned.

"All the work!" he sounded dejected.

"I'm only kidding; I like to forge her handwriting."

"If you want, you can decide what kind of flowers to plant."

"Roses, Henrietta wouldn't mind if we put in roses."

"What about Arp. Won't he be coming around to get leaves from the garden?"

"He can have leaves; it'll just be the ones we pick. All we have to do is mix some of ours in with the dried ones." A fanciful gleam fell over Yoshi's entire expression. "His days as a roreg will be short-lived."

"Sort of like a bartender watering down the vodka!" laughed Saachi. "He'll get mad."

"At who, we're just a pair of dumb kids! What's he gonna do to us? Tell our mother!" The absurdity of their situation hastily turned into comic relief. They didn't feel the gravity of the situation nor any resentment towards Henrietta. She had been a caricature of a mother, and they had become the cartoonist in charge of the pen and ink.

"Let's order Chinese and get enough for the dragon," Saachi said.

"That a great idea. I'll order lots just in case someone might come by; then, we'll have enough."

"Like that dumb Sikes?" she scowled.

"No, not him. I saw him at the library and pretty sure he's not coming around anymore."

"That's good."

"There are others like us you know."

"I remember, that's what you said." Saachi got up and walked over to the window. "I think I'll go to the beach," she said and pulled the drapes aside and sat down.

There was a quiet in his head that he didn't recognize. He closed his eyes. The image of The Colony appeared. Frito, Hawk, Kobo, Ivan, Gustave, and some other small boy. *What's your name, kid? Iago. Welcome, Iago. Welcome to The Colony.*

Rule #1 Kinship is to protect, Rule #2 Doing evil is not always evil…